GHOSTLY

HOWLS

GHOSTLY HOWLS

Stephanie Hansen

HYPOTHESIS

BOOKS

ISBN 9781735042350
1 2 3 4 5 6 7 8 9 10
Printed in the U.S.A.
First printing, 2022

The text type was set in Perpetua and Times New Roman.

Cover design by MiblArt

For those who dare to follow their dreams and never look back.

CHAPTER ONE—ORLA

"The world is full of magic things, patiently waiting for our senses to grow sharper."
William Butler Yeats

Being a soul possessor can be unpleasant. Everyone's emotions cry out to me like children waiting to be found in a game of Marco Polo. At least Dave gets that I don't like to be touched (it's what triggers possession of the soul, but he doesn't know that part). He keeps his distance though sometimes I wish he didn't. He's across the marina with his crew, celebrating a successful hoist net catch from earlier today. The setting sun paints every wave like an instant chocolate hard shell on ice cream.

There's been a steady stream of gatherings on Wharf Road downtown since fishing has been good. Our town is so tiny that any party spilling out of a house is noteworthy. Ethel, VA, isn't known for its numbers, with a population under a thousand. The only people who realize Ben has the maritime museum literally in his house are all locals. Tourists are few and far between. Our parties may be small, but they are mighty. Blame it on our Irish roots and the bagpipes every now and then.

The crisp fall wind whips through my hair as I stand dockside with a customer. She's been looking at cockles for the past ten minutes like a lost puppy. I've waited patiently for her to ask me questions, but it seems I may have to approach her in order for that to happen. A look of relief washes across her face as I approach, and she goes to grab my hand, touching it ever so slightly. A tickle scurries its way up my arm, but I retract my hand until the final spiritual string reverberates back with a shock. I don't want to possess the spirit of this woman. I only want her to buy a few cockles.

"Orla, is that your name?" the woman asks, snapping me back to attention, to this world. "Did you hear me? I would like to know if the grit has been washed off of these."

She's unfamiliar with the process. These are fresh. She'll want to soak them in salted water overnight before she prepares them. That will remove the grit. Probably doesn't even know to throw away the ones that open by morning. But perhaps she's distracted. A bit of pain singed my arm when her hand brushed against mine.

"Have you ever prepared cockles before?" I ask her.

She rolls her eyes at me.

"I have a cockle recipe book with instructions available for only five dollars," I say.

"Never mind," she huffs and walks away. I notice a trifold pamphlet jutting out of her purse. All I can read is *Cockles May Cure Cancer Naturally*. That was the misery I felt when I had been so close to possessing her spirit. Cancer sucks.

"Ma'am," I shout after her. "Please, this bucket of cockles and the book is on the house."

She turns back to me. Her forehead scrunches as she takes a deep breath. "Fine."

At her car door, she grabs the book from my outstretched hand and shoves it into her purse. As her Jeep drives away, I hope the pamphlet's right.

"You're not going to make any money giving inventory away for free," Dave says as he approaches. His broad shoulders block the sun out of my eyes. I smile wishing I'd done more than throw my thick, long hair up in a ponytail today. I might be wrong, but I think I see a hint of blush in his cheeks as our eyes lock.

"Yeah, what's it to you?" I turn to close up shop like Dave and his crew have already done.

He waits for me because he's my ride home. We've been friends since we were kids. It's not uncommon in this small town, but I wish we could be more. I wish I could touch others without possessing their soul. I would feel safe in Dave's arms. There's been a tension around us lately like he wants to be close too, but there's a constant buffer, poking fun, and egging each other on, neither of us knowing how long it can last or if and when one of us will succumb.

"Have you caught the latest rumor?" Dave laughs. His dimples can't help but show when he smirks.

"What are they saying now?"

"A few from Oliver's crew claim to be hearing voices at night."

"I'm surprised you don't all hear voices at night, what with the hours of sun you get and only drinking whiskey or beer instead of water most of the time."

"Hey, layoff, would ya? Anyhoo, I guess these voices have been asking for their papers—saying they shouldn't have docked without them."

"Sounds like they've been out at sea too long."

"Whatever. Don't believe if you don't want to."

Only then do I recognize the shakiness in his voice. He rubs the back of his neck nervously. These rumors must really be getting to him. "Want to swing by the pub on the way home?"

That brings a smile back to his face. The pub's in the heart of downtown, where the roads are brick, and each store or restaurant has its own unique awning. In this small town, it's where neighboring businesses get each other's mail when someone's away and where people watch out for one another like a family...most of the time.

Beside me, his jacket is stretched across his shoulders, and it's so easy, too easy, to remember what he looks like without a shirt on. I take a deep breath and try to steady my nerves as we walk to his truck.

"Think Molly will be there?" he asks.

"Does a fish swim?" I joke. "Yeah, it's her shift."

"Think she might be in the mood to hand out inventory for free too?"

I move to swat his arm with the back of my hand but catch myself before I do. I've never had so much trouble keeping my hands to myself. There's an awkward tension in the air between us again. Luckily, we have to step away from each other as I enter the passenger side and he enters the driver's side of his old, rusty pickup but then we'll be close again.

We pass by the lighthouse during our seaside drive. It's on a small island just off the mainland. As kids, we called it Alcatraz. Air escapes my nose as I silently laugh, but Dave's too into finding music on the radio to notice. We used to pretend we were going to swim there and release the prisoners by mapping out the best escape route and guard shift changes.

Now the sun is setting behind the structure. It's white and tall, looking like a space shuttle ready to depart from the Kennedy Space Center in Florida. That was another fun game. I would disappear, and Dave would radio directions as if he were ground control. I look at the lighthouse one last time before it's out of view and notice a shadow in the lantern room. It's almost like someone walking across, but that can't be. The lighthouse hasn't operated in a long time. I lean forward to get a better view through the truck window.

The truck comes to an abrupt stop as Dave pulls over to the side of the road. Sea droplets spray in through the window, sprinkling against me, dampening my arm.

"You saw it too," he proclaims.

"Saw what, Dave?"

"You can't make fun of Oliver's crew's rumors anymore."

I raise my eyebrows and nod.

"You have to believe the ghost stories now." He points to the lighthouse.

"Perhaps an animal has finally made its way in there."

"You're unbelievable," he says while pulling back onto the road. "You never believe in anything supernatural."

The rest of the drive is devoid of conversation. What would he do if he knew that a supernatural was sitting right next to him? While Dave's always read that I have an aversion to touch, I've never flat out told him why and he's continued to respect my privacy. Maybe he's a supernatural with an abnormal power to resist temptation.

I continue my staring out the window, now free of ghostly disturbances. Docks and the beach, pass but before we make it into town, I catch sight of a group of kids racing their model sailboats. Dave and I exchange a wistful look. So many memories float around this town, like the attic of a grandparent's house. It's easy to feel at home here no matter where you go. And yet, I've never really felt that I belonged either. I give Dave a closed-mouth smile before turning away so he can't see the look of isolated pain.

9

We pass by green, striped, and even metal awnings before arriving at Shabby Tabby. There's a long table for large parties as you walk in to the right of the bar. Then four-person tables litter the somewhat open area. The arched ceilings have led me to believe Shabby Tabby was not always a pub. Outside are more four-person tables under a deck glittered with globe lights above and below.

We take our normal stools at the bar. I notice the outdoor light glint off of Molly's red hair. I wave to get her attention, but before I'm able to tell if she saw me, Russ, a regular, stumbles into my back. The connection's automatic. I'm in his mind, and he's in mine, but I'm the only one who has a clue of what's going on and any ability to control things in our space now. His thoughts bounce around his head like a pinball machine. Is this what it's like for Russ when he's drunk? The thoughts are of doubt and despair. I know he's had it rough losing his job and going through a divorce.

I project thoughts of my own before pulling away, ones of positivity about how he'll rebuild himself and be there for his daughter.

"You okay, Russ?" I ask as he rights himself on the stool next to me.

"Yeah." He pauses, scratching the stubble on his cheek. "Yeah, actually, I'm good. Haven't felt this way in ages."

Oh, Russ. Hopefully, the positive thoughts can help him and turn his thinking in a better direction than it has been.

Dave clears his throat. "Be careful where you walk, would ya, Russ." The knuckles holding his mug of beer are white due to his grip being so tight.

"It's not a big deal," I say under my breath to Dave, hoping he hasn't spun Russ back to a place of negativity while also trying to ward off the splitting headache attempting to take residence in my head.

But Russ doesn't seem to be bothered at all. In fact, he gets up and practically skips out of the pub.

"What's that guy's problem? Did he hurt you?"

"No, I'm fine. Did you order my usual?"

Kyle, the bartender, brings me a Jameson on the rocks, answering my question. I'll just have the one. That's all I ever have, and tend to drink a lot of water at the same time. I never want to lose my composure again. Not like I did a few years ago at age twenty-two. It was awful when Molly had to take care of me while I was drunk. She had to hold me up, and we were in each other's minds, but I was without my usual control and clarity. It was almost bad enough that neither of us could surface. Thank goodness we did. I learned my lesson to never be drunk again. But it's nice to be able to take the edge off. Just a little bit of alcohol allows me to sleep without the thoughts, dreams, and nightmares of those I've possessed haunting me each night.

As Molly approaches us, I think about how she's the only one who can truly understand that side of me. She has powers of her own. It's similar to the old Irish folklore tale of the banshees but opposite because she's a halfling. Instead of screaming out awful noises when death is near, Molly hears them. Sometimes it's specified to when certain people are near, those within weeks of dying. Other times it can be more generalized, meaning all she knows is that there will be a death nearby soon and nothing further. Her ability can reach miles out, which is why being in a small town is beneficial to her. Otherwise, if she were in a large city, she'd probably hear ringing all the time. Her gift plagues her just as much as mine plagues me. Which is one reason why we've been best friends for so long and are now roommates.

"You two need to hit the showers," she says to Dave and me. "You reek of fish."

"This whole town smells of the sea, silly," I quip back.

"Oh, the odor of stale Guinness and cigar smoke is better?" Dave raises an eyebrow.

She playfully jabs him in the arm.

"You hear from Cormac yet?" I ask.

"No," Molly kicks up some dust from the floor. "It's been radio silence."

"Hey, wanna shoot some pool?" Dave asks. "That will keep your mind off it."

"Thanks, but my shift's about up."

"I can walk home with you," I offer to which Dave curls his lip in a mock pout.

"Yeah, you wouldn't want the ghost to get her," Dave says.

"What ghost?"

"Don't listen to him."

"Okay?"

Silence descends upon us as Molly helps clean a few glasses, and then turns in her portion of the tips to the kitchen crew. She's rushing through everything and I'm not sure if it's simply that her shift was subpar or if, like me, she's experiencing a strange foreboding.

CHAPTER TWO—MOLLY
"We learn from failure, not from success!"
Abraham (Bram) Stoker

It feels bad taking Orla away from Dave, but I need to talk to her.

"What ghost was Dave talking about?" I ask Orla as soon as we're outside.

"Don't listen to Dave," she says while running a hand through her hair. "We just saw the shadow from an animal in the lighthouse lantern room."

"Really? He's usually not one to be easily spooked."

"Yeah, but I guess Oliver's crew has been hearing voices or something."

A shudder runs through her, and she quickens her step. I have to lengthen my strides to keep up. Thoughts bounce around in my head as we walk in silence while I try to distract myself and, of course, images of Cormac invade my mind.

Cormac's perfect, in my humble opinion. Her eyes crinkle when she smiles, and her face is full of light despite the broodiness she tries to exude. I can't believe I got mad at her last week. Once again, my demon self appeared, thanks to my good ol' friend Jameson. Not the person but the Irish Whiskey! Sometimes I wonder if being half banshee means the banshee side always wins. I just wish Cormac would text me back already.

To move my desperate thoughts to something, anything else I think of my other plans. I can't wait to get home and add my tips to my savings. Pretty soon, I'll be able to afford the next piece of my sleeve tattoo. It's a mix of roses and Celtic symbols. Orla seems to have a glow about her even though I can tell she's trying to hide it from me as we walk home. I hope she will tell Dave about her ability. He would totally work with her to make a relationship happen. I think he's loved her since he found out what love is. It's probably why he's had a rebel streak, unrequited love.

"Sell a lot of cockles today?" I ask Orla.

"It was decent," she responds. "Gave some away free too."

"Hey, we need to pay rent. You can't be doing that."

"No, this lady, she has cancer."

"I didn't hear any piercing ringing today. She'll be fine…at least for now."

"Maybe cockles really do cure cancer. See, you should be eating them more often."

"I live near them. Their smell permeates my pores. They're not getting more than that."

As we approach our home, I take it all in yet again. Never did I think I'd be in a house of my own, well, mine and Orla's. We did have a third roommate for a very short time. Jenny never does stay in one place for long. It even has a second story. Sure the paint is chipping here and there, but the entry is through an arched doorway. How badass is that? The windows have shutters. The first thing viewable once inside is the massive staircase screaming just how gigantic, at least to me, this place is. Orla and I have split the floor-to-ceiling bookshelves in the living room. Her half is full of romance and fantasy, while my side is full of thrillers and horror. There are hardwood floors throughout. The only thing I haven't been able to determine is the concealed door at the end of the hallway upstairs. Where does it go? We haven't been able to locate its key.

"Boomer," Orla says as we enter, and our border collie beagle mix runs up to greet her. She bends over so she can pet him. It's good for her to have a pet, something she can touch without possessing its soul. I'm not sure why dogs and cats are safe from her power, but I'm glad she can at least have the outlet free of obstacles.

"He needs a bath."

She nods in agreement. "Wanna work on our puzzle in a bit?"

"Maybe," I say. "Or we could do a reading."

"Sure. I'll settle in and brew some tea."

Cormac's perfume hits me the second I open the door to my room. She's not here, unfortunately. It's just left over. She always places a hand on my cheek before she's going to kiss me. I like that. I miss it. Her hand would then snake its way around to the back of my neck and grab my hair as we were kissing. For a moment, it would feel as though I wasn't damaged goods. I check my phone for the hundredth time but nothing's there.

She'd been the only one to look at me that way as if I had a clean slate. As if my past screw-ups were nonexistent. It's not that I mean to mess it up all the time. Just like tattoos help me not focus on the pain I feel inside, getting drunk and acting a fool erases tortures from the past, if only for a fleeting moment.

A cold draft flows through my room, sending tingles up my neck. I hear a crackle pop. It's not the ringing I usually hear, but it's from within, like the ringing. Next, a low voice whispers, *Drogheda*. I tremor, trying to shake the ominous feeling. I've never heard a voice before.

"Orla," I yell. "Orla."

"What?" She's panting when she barges through my door. "What is it?"

"Did you hear that?"

"Oh, no."

"It's not that," I pause, unsure of how to proceed. "I…I heard a voice."

"What did it say?"

"I'm not sure…Dragon. No…Drogen."

"Weird. That's a new one."

"Yeah."

"You okay?"

I shrug.

"The tea's ready. Let's go have it while it's warm."

Orla has always used tea to soothe me when I'm upset. My favorite being the orange-flavored teas because I love the tangy taste. As we descend the stairs, I can't help but be glad we live together. I no longer have to face things alone. Most people have to visit their grandparents to see a puzzle mid-process on the dining room table. I just have to walk downstairs.

"Want to work on the puzzle before the reading?" I ask her, knowing the answer. It should help calm my nerves a bit.

"Of course," she responds.

"I'll grab the tea and be right back."

Walking to the kitchen, I hear the same crackle pop again, like raindrops falling on my eardrum. Unsure of how to proceed or what might come next, I slowly enter the kitchen, pausing with each step. A floor-board creaks, not from behind me where Orla is in the dining room and not from underneath me, but in front of me. Boomer's nowhere to be seen, probably by my room-mate's side. What could that have been?

A breeze rolls through the kitchen even though no door or window is ajar. Papers rustle, and towels move. I take the remaining couple of steps to the kettle as quickly as I can. When I place my hand on it, the room around me fades away, and I'm immersed into a scene from centuries before.

Old rickety wagons roll across a dirt street but what catches my attention most is the prisoner bound in rope awaiting execution. When her eyes lock with mine, I recognize them immediately…it's Cormac. I reach for her, but the executioner gets there first. I hear the voice again, *Drogheda*.

"Molly," Orla shouts while snapping her fingers in front of my face.

"What?"

"You didn't hear the kettle ring out even though it was right next to you. If you didn't answer for another two-seconds, I was going to slap you."

"I'm okay." I take a deep breath, trying to relax. I pick up the tea kettle and return to the dining room, grabbing two mugs from the hutch cabinet before sitting down. I'm really not ready to talk about what I just saw.

"What was it? First, Dave's claiming to have seen a ghost, and now you look like you've been visited by one."

"I need to think about anything else for a bit. I did see something, but I'm not ready to talk about it." My leg bounces as I sit.

"We can work on the puzzle," she says and smiles while pouring our tea. Boomer paces around the table before sitting on the dog bed we have placed in the corner.

I find a puzzle piece that fits just inside the border, put it in place, and take a deep breath. "Did you hear the word about Kyle?"

"Bartender Kyle?" Orla asks as she raises her eyebrows.

"He finally proposed to Ben."

"It's about time."

"I know, right? There are going to be two bests of honor, and I'm one of them."

"You hate dresses."

"Duh, Kyle would never."

"Ever rent a tux?"

"Yeah, no biggie…but I need your help."

"With what?"

"Planning the No Longer Single party."

Orla rubs her hands together, already scheming ideas.

"Does Ben now have help at the museum so they can take a proper honeymoon?"

I nod my head, yes.

She fits another piece into the puzzle. "As excited as I am for Kyle and Ben, will you please let me know what happened in the kitchen earlier?"

I let out a shaky breath.

"I think I had a vision."

"Really?" Orla grabs the tarot deck and holds it in the smoke from the sage incense on the table for a bit.

"Yeah, it was like from the past."

"Interesting." She shuffles the cards in her way, making multiple piles and then picking them up.

"Cormac was in it too."

"Hm, she has been on your mind a lot lately." I pull three cards, cutting with my left hand and picking up the top with my right.

24

"She was bound in rope."

Once the cards are face down, Orla turns them over one by one as she considers what I've said. The first card is the right-side-up knight of pentacles. "Looks like it's hard work for us ahead."

"But what do you think the rope means?"

"I'm hoping the cards tell us."

The second card is an upside-down six of cups. "Maybe your vision means you need to let Cormac go."

I huff. That can't be it. I felt an immediate urgency with the vision, far from a peaceful letting it go sense.

The final card is an upside-down six of wands. "Molly, do you love Cormac?"

"What?"

"You can't live your whole life rejecting love."

"I'm not…."

"You're going to need to accept it and tell her that you love her."

"Or, she'll be executed?"

"What?"

"That's what happened in the vision."

"Maybe if you don't tell her, she'll miss out on her only chance to love too?"

I take a sip of tea to process this information. Orla knows me better than anyone. Could she be right? It's still not sitting well with me. I wish Cormac would just text me back already. I wave the burning sage over the cards to cleanse them.

"Your turn," I tell Orla.

CHAPTER THREE—ORLA

"As you ramble through life, whatever be
your goal;
keep your eye upon the doughnut, and not
upon the hole." Irish Saying

Watching her closely, I notice Molly's
hand shaking as she circles the cards
through the sage smoke. The herbaceous
scent prickles my nose. I made light of her
vision using the cards because I don't want
to alarm her. She's been through enough
trauma, and nothing serious has been con-
firmed. Yeah, Oliver's crew is seeing
ghosts *And* Dave thinks we saw one in the
lighthouse. The timing of Cormac's being
missing in action and the occurrences are a
little unsettling but add Molly's vision on
top of it, and I'm downright worried.

She shuffles the traditional way, bridge
and all. It might be one of the only traditional things about her. After placing the
three cards I drew face down on the table.
She makes eye contact with me. Concern

misting through her gaze, I can see my making light of things didn't completely work for her either. I should have known because it never really does, but it hasn't kept me from trying yet.

Her hand hovers over the cards like each carry the direction our lives are about to take. The first card she turns over is a tower.

"Disaster?" she asks with concern.

All I can do is nod as I gulp, leery of what's to come next.

The following card she turns over is the reversed six of wands.

"Punishment?" I ask, confused. "Was the execution you saw in your vision a punishment?"

Instead of light coming into Molly's eyes, it's as if hers goes out like with every finding her gaze becomes more of a dull stare, lost beyond belief.

"Are you okay?" I ask her.

Now she nods and then turns over the final card. It's a reversed sun.

"Sadness," she says. The tears in her eyes reflect the candlelight. I'm stunned only for a second, but then I grab all of the cards from her as well as the lighter by the incense and slowly but meticulously burn them, letting the soot fall onto a plate.

"Wait, what are you doing?" she asks.

"We need a purification after that."

"Okay, but I can't shake the feeling that all of the instances today have some sort of deeper meaning. Shouldn't we look into that?"

"I'm listening." But also continuing to incinerate these rotten cards. Warmth tingles my fingers tips, and I drop a lit card watching it burn completely to ash.

"Ghosts, visions, and bad readings," she muses.

"I'm not sure what to think about the ghosts." I shrug my shoulders. "What was the word you heard in the vision?"

"Drogheda," she says with a look on her face like it just clicked.

"Does it mean something to you?"

29

"I think it's historical."

We both pull out our phones and begin searching for Drogheda.

"It's in Ireland." I turn my phone her way.

"There was a siege there." She shows me her phone too. I see the site she's found and pull it up on my phone as well. The siege occurred September 11th, 1649. When the town didn't surrender, it was stormed. Executions occurred not only of militia... but also civilians.

"That's creepy." I look at my friend with astonishment.

"Yeah, but I still don't get what it means."

I pull out a map from the hutch drawer. The town handed these out at the fair last year. I don't know why I kept it, but I think it might be able to help us now. I grab a blue pen and put a star at Shabby Tabby's location. Then a star at the lighthouse.

"What are you doing?" Molly has joined me on this side of the table and is leaning over the map.

"You met Cormac at the bar, right."

"Yes."

"And we saw the ghost at the light-house."

"Okay."

"I'm marking the spots of locations that might be important to figuring out what's going on."

"Cormac and I often went to Queen's Chalet."

I star it on the map. "I thought that place was abandoned."

"Perfect spot for privacy." She shrugs.

"I wish I knew where Oliver's crew saw ghosts too."

"Do you know what day it was? Or, what fishing route had been scheduled?"

"No, but I know who would." I pull out my phone and text Dave. My foot taps nervously under the table as we await his response. Once I have the coordinates, I add them to the map.

"It almost forms a circle, but it's not complete yet. We should go there, to the missing spot."

"Uh, it's pretty dark. I don't think we'd be able to see much."

"But, what if Cormac's there?" Molly's hunched a little, biting her fingernails, and then her hands go to her ears. "Wait, I hear ringing." Her hands are shaking.

Just then, my phone rings, and we both jump. It's Dave. I answer the phone. "Hey, what's up?"

"You have to come," he says.

"Where? Why?"

"Bethel's Landing." There's a pause, and for a moment, I think I've lost connection, but then I hear Dave's breath, and the foreboding feeling has rolled up with desperation. Bethel's Landing is in the direct vicinity of the missing spot on our circle. "They've found a body."

*****

I try to keep Molly calm as we watch for Dave's truck, but that proves to be an impossible task. She paces back and forth in our small living room until headlights flood the space in artificial light.

"Took you long enough," she tells Dave once we're in the truck.

"What's with her?" he asks.

"Don't ask," I say. "Just get us to the water."

Normally, police wouldn't allow civilians near crime scenes, but in our small town, they've realized our appearance is unavoidable. They set up safe areas nearby for us instead though usually, our crime scenes are not related to dead bodies. A crowd has already formed when we arrive. There are lights set up toward the water's edge so investigators can see. It looks like a creepy photo shoot with what can only be a body on the ground. I can't tell anything beyond that it appears to be human.

Molly breathes in a sigh of relief. "It's not her. She never wears anything but black."

Maybe the visions were just that. I wish I could hug Molly right now. The blue jeans and green shirt are fading in color as if their life is draining along with the body itself. It sends a wave of dizziness through me, but I take a deep breath before stars can encroach on my vision. I cannot faint here. Someone would for sure try to catch me in this crowd, and it's hard enough to keep my distance, so no one touches me as it is.

"Cormac's a tough one. You shouldn't worry so much." Dave gives her the side hug that I can't.

I'm still uneasy with all of the recent occurrences. A flash pulls my eyes back to the body. Someone from forensics with gloves on their hands circles the corpse like a vulture looking for a meal. Different plastic evidence tents with numbers are placed all around like restaurant waiting queues. I double over, putting my hands on my knees for support.

"Are you okay?" Dave gives me a worried look.

"Hey, Chica!" I recognize the voice behind us immediately, and my worry shifts to Molly. Dave and I simultaneously turn around as if we have the same shared thought. Cormac's back!

Despite how angry she should be and how mad I know she is, Molly envelops Cormac in a vice-like hug. "You're okay," is all she's able to mutter out in disbelief.

"Yeah, everything's cool." Cormac pats Molly's back.

Molly tenses, and I know my strong friend's spine has returned. She shoves Cormac away. "Why didn't you answer my texts or my calls? Where have you been?"

Cormac runs a hand through her hair. Just then, Oliver strolls up behind her, and a tremor runs its way up my body. Dave gives me another concerned look and then turns to Oliver. Dave's jaw clenches in anger, but it's nothing compared to the fumes running out of Molly as Oliver steps far too much inside Cormac's personal space.

"She's been helping us out at sea," Oliver says, and then he smirks at Cormac.

I swear Molly is about to be charged with assault because she looks like she could kill Oliver right now, even though we're surrounded by cops.

"What were you doing out to sea?" Molly asks Cormac, releasing her anger and instead throwing care Cormac's way. Damn if she doesn't have a talent for reading a situation and one upping a predator.

"They've been seeing things, and you know I have a direct line of communication with the afterlife." Cormac's eyes plead to Molly. "I thought I could help."

Cormac's belief is sweet but nowhere near what Molly and I have to deal with. Why couldn't she have texted Molly to let her know? Something's fishy, and it's not the usual Ethel smell. There's something

36

going on, and I need to find out what it is. But Molly's hugging Cormac again then they're kissing.

"Want to go to your place?"

"Sure." Cormac smiles slyly and waves goodbye.

I watch the pair walk away, worried for my friend but knowing full well there's nothing I can say right now that would stop her.

Dave shrugs and then looks back at the body.

"See, I think our sightings mean more than you give them credit," Oliver says to Dave, pointing toward the body.

I feel the color drain out of my face as I look back that way because now they're zipping up a bag around the corpse. There will be no reviving for that soul. It was abandoned out here probably by its killer.

"Even Orla believes," Oliver says as he steps closer to me.

Dave juts between us. "I think it's time for you to go home, Oliver."

The two men stare each other down for a beat, and then Oliver surrenders, turning away. As he leaves, the tremor that had gone through me before returns, but now it's a tremble. Once Oliver's headlights are fully out of view, Dave pivots to me.

"How about I take you home now?"

I nod in relief. The entire ride is full of tension. There's so much I want to tell him. I want to tell him about Molly's visions. I want to tell him about the foreboding feeling. I want to tell him everything but I can't. He keeps stealing glances in my direction, sensing my strain.

Once back at the house, he kills the engine and walks me in, which isn't entirely out of character, yet it feels different, stronger. As soon as the door closes, my emotions cut loose like an ocean wave crashing into me, the current sucking me under.

"Damn it, I know you don't like to be touched." Dave clenches and unclenches his fists. "Our whole lives you've avoided touching anyone even though it caused you to be ostracized as a kid AND ever since apart from a loyal few. But I need to comfort you. It's beyond my control."

"I want you to comfort me too," I whisper, and he takes two massive steps, closing the distance between us. His arms wrap around me with his chin set atop my head. For one fraction of the most blissful moment, warmth engulfs me stripping away my fear, pain, and hurt. All too quickly, it's over, and I'm possessing the soul of the only man I've ever loved.

CHAPTER FOUR—MOLLY

"Keep love in your heart. A life without it
is like a sunless garden when the flowers
are all dead." Oscar Wilde

Cormac leads the way into her apartment,
holding my hand, and my mind flashes
back to when we first met. Her band per-
forms regularly at Shabby Tabby ever since
they moved into town. Part of me wanted to
keep my distance, guessing that they'd be
relocating before too long. The other part of
me couldn't keep away. After a guy in the
crowd leaned in and tried to grope her while
she was singing, I'd been sure to only sit
safe customers within reaching distance of
her. She'd noticed when it'd happened a
couple nights in a row and nodded at me in
appreciation. And then she smiled. It was
like a light shining through her perfectly
parted, blonde hair. A dimple surfaced in
her right cheek alongside her crooked
smile. It gave her smooth as silk skin character and instantly warmed my heart.

Still, I never thought I'd have a chance. I'm sure she saw enough troublemakers in her line of work. I'd just be another one hitting on her. So, I continued to keep my distance. But one day, as I was clearing a table, a pair of hands with chipped forest green nail polish and goth rings appeared before me. Cormac was leaning on the table. "When's your shift up? Want to go grab a cup o' joe?" she'd asked me.

At first, my breath had been so lost I couldn't speak to answer, and then, like the fool that I am, I began nodding "yes" as if this would impress her. I quickly regained my senses and said, "Yeah, I'd love that. You been to the Daily Grind yet?"

After my shift, she waved off her fellow band members, walked up to me, and latched one of her arms in mine, and I've been locked ever since. That is until, after months of being attached at the hip, she decided to leave me hanging and not answer any of my texts or calls. I should ask her more about what she was doing with

Oliver's crew and why she didn't reach out, but that could derail our current forward movement, and it's just not worth it to me. Once we're in the kitchen, she lets go so she can grab two mugs and turn on the coffee maker. We've had many cups of joe since that first one. It's one of our favorite pastimes.

"You sure it's okay that I'm here?" I ask.

"Where else would you be?" Cormac cocks her eyebrow.

"It's a quick jump from the silent treatment."

"We're just making coffee."

"We never just have coffee."

"I restocked your favorite Daily Grind blend." The thought warms me.

"Bet you got their additives too."

I grab her hips from behind to move her out of the way so I can get the sugar and cream. Before she steps to the side, she turns in my direction. Now my hands are on her hips as she faces me, locking her eyes

42

with mine. She puts her arms over my shoulders, and our lips crush together. The kiss is full of passion and urgency. Maybe she missed me as much as I missed her. My breath quickens, and I'm lost. Pulling off her jacket, I lean into her against the pantry door. She's unbuckling my belt and pulling it through the loops. It rubs my skin and burns, but nothing's felt so good.

I reach under her shirt, touching her perfect body. She's a mixture of boniness in some spots while ample in others. It gets me panting just remembering how she feels. Then her hands are down my jeans, and she brushes her fingers over my hips. Her supple hands move fluidly to the spots of most pleasure but stop before fully engaging. I lift her shirt moving close enough that I can feel my breath bounce off her skin and back onto my face. I softly rub my hands over the tips of her chest in the paper-thin, smooth motion that I know is excruciatingly wonderful. She groans.

I kiss her neck and behind her ear. I think I might just lose myself in the jungle of her hair. Her skin is warm and smooth, and has all the comfort I need right now. How I've missed this. She's like the caffeine I'm addicted to, a pain when missing but sweet, sweet serenity once I consume her. She pushes her body against mine, rubbing in a rhythmic dance of need. And just as we're about to remove articles of clothing and bring each other to a climax, I open my eyes to look at her, but the image I expect to see isn't there. In its place is the scene of Cormac tied and ready for execution.

With a sharp intake of breath, I step back, my heart pounding, pulsing in the most quenchable parts of my body.

"What," she sputters out. "What are you doing?" She reaches to pull me back to her.

I reciprocate with a fiercely strong hug.

"I have to tell you something," I say into her hair.

"Can't it wait?"

"No, listen. I think you're in danger."

Now she nudges me away to look into my eyes.

"What are you talking about? Don't be upset about me hanging out with Oliver. He's harmless."

"No, that's not it. You know what, never mind."

"Huh, no. You do not get to just drop this."

"Okay, I've been seeing these visions. I just saw one."

"Oh, but why push me away?"

"In my visions, you're bound...awaiting execution."

"Seriously, why not protect me."

"That's what I'm trying to do. You can't go out on Oliver's ship again."

She picks up her jacket.

"Where are you going?"

"Why do you think I didn't tell you about being out with Oliver's crew, to begin with?"

She walks to the door and opens it.

"You're leaving me in your apartment?"

"You know how to lock up."

And with that, she's gone. How frustrating! I need her to listen to me. How am I going to protect her when she's keeping away from me? How can we be so hot one minute and then cold the next? I need to get my stuff together. It's time to go talk to Kyle.

*****

"This is your fourth. Maybe you should slow down."

"I'm fine, Kyle. Everything's fine."

"Perhaps some rest would be good."

"Why does she keep leaving?"

"She's been helping Oliver's crew with ghosts."

"Do you actually think that's what Oliver's doing? It seems like something he typically ignores."

"Oliver isn't usually one to believe, but this time seems to have shaken him."

"Tell me more about Cormac's direct line of communication with the dead."

"They're not dead to her."

"What are they then?"

"Cormac believes our souls take a pause in an afterlife place before being reincarnated."

"Okay. She's never talked to me about that."

"Guess it never came up."

Kyle serves Claire from the café a couple barstools away, and a few of Cormac's song lyrics float through my head like a fog over the morning water. *Our souls exist forever intertwined,* makes my heart pound, and *your essence will haunt me eternally* has my palms sweating. Then I remember hearing *Drogheda* and the research with Orla unveiling an event centuries ago. Someone lost the woman they loved. Every time I see the vision, I can feel their ache in the pit of my stomach.

Speaking of stomach, I need to put some solid food in mine. I must sober up and figure out what the hell is going on. I pull up more articles on the siege of Drogheda and, as I'm reading stumble upon the story of two lovers escaping an Irish castle only to be lost at sea. Rumor has it that she's now a banshee who haunts the castle on stormy nights. My being half banshee doesn't calm my nerves, but the smell of purple onions on a club sandwich overrides my trepidation, and I devour it as quickly as I can.

I need to know what's happening with Cormac and Oliver. What is their crew really seeing? And who is Cormac communicating with? I'm going to have to ask something of Orla I never ask…for her to use her power. All she'd have to do is put a hand on Cormac's shoulder. She'd be able to see everything so clearly, and we could sort all of this out. She's able to use my power any day she wants. I don't have the leisure of turning mine off. She can avoid hers by not touching anyone. I hear the ringing no matter what I do so long as death is around.

Sometimes I like being in a small town because there's less ringing. Other times it's worse. I knew before we lost Elma from the bakery, remembering how she offered me free breakfast growing up. Not everyone but a few very special people have become close. Losing them is worse. Knowing when they're about to die is devastating.

I take the last bite of my sandwich and pull a wad of cash out of my pocket. Setting it on the bar I yell, "Thanks, Kyle! Good luck with the wedding plans."

"Yeah, too bad Jenny's no longer in town. She was exceptionally good at making floral arrangements." He waves, and I leave, wishing I had on more than a jacket. The wind bites through the thin material, and I shiver. Walking home, I fear the reprimand I'm going to receive. Orla will have expected me to demand an explanation, and apology from Cormac, but instead, all I could do was think that she was safe and having the warmth of her body up against mine. Hopefully, Dave has kept Orla preoccupied. I wish they'd work through her barriers already. I'm tired of seeing her sad looks when she thinks no one's watching. Staring out into the sky as if it holds some answer she's yet to discover. How the first second when she sees him, she lights up, but it's quickly dashed with anguish. I've been so worried about Cormac. Have I dropped the ball not worrying for my best friend, the one who has always been there for me? Is she okay?

All of a sudden, it feels as if a pair of eyes must be watching me. I quicken my step, remembering the corpse we saw at Bethel's Landing. Why did the ringing not give me more heads-up notice? Am I losing my touch? Would I hear ringing if I were about to die? My eyes dart from one shadowed spot to another, expecting something to jump out at any second. Who was it at Bethel's Landing? I'd been so preoccupied with Cormac and the visions that I forgot to find out. Murder has come to our small town. It lingers around my head like smoke from a tobacco pipe, close and persistent. The silence is creepy once I finally reach our house. I don't even hear Boomer's whining or barks. My hands shake as I retrieve my keys, and it takes three tries before unlocking our door...

CHAPTER FIVE—ORLA

"It's my rule never to lose my temper till it would be detrimental to keep it." Seán O'Casey

Possessing the soul of the only man I've ever loved has its perks. In Dave's mind, I see him imagining our first kiss. He's grabbing my hair as our bodies are like magnets pulling us into one another. Then he moves one hand to my hip and the other to the nape of my neck while he kisses below my ear on the opposite side. I gasp even though these are only thoughts. He physically gasps realizing, that I'm inside his head, but he doesn't let go. To be fair, I push forward one of my own thoughts, so it's an equal invasion of privacy. In the vision, I lift my head, giving him more access to my throat, and moan. I push forward the tingling sensation on my hip where he's touching it so that the tingling spreads to his hand. It's everything I've hoped for and more.

"What? How?" he asks silently in our heads like he's a pro at this.

"I'm a soul possessor, Dave. I possess anyone I touch."

"That's why…"

"Yes."

"I don't care. I don't want you to go another day untouched."

"I can see your every secret."

"And?"

"It's rude. It's not fair."

He closes the spiritual space that formed between us for conversation, and we're kissing again, both in our minds and not. I wrap my arms around his neck. I can feel every muscle in his chest as he reaches his arms around me, his biceps pressing into my sides. Our mouths seem to be molded for this, a perfect fit. His tongue is a mix of strength and gentleness with years of passion behind it. My breaths quicken. Our lips separate for just a second to catch our breath.

And that's when it suddenly goes all wrong. I see his recent bursts of anger and realize they were out of his control. Something's been bothering him lately, and not even he knows what it is. He sees what I'm seeing and pushes physically away from me, panic streaking through his eyes. So not the pro at soul surrender I'd hoped he'd be. It leaves me with a cold and lonely space.

"Is everything okay?"

He seems so lost.

"Yeah." He clears his throat. "All good. That was intense."

"I know."

He turns to leave, looking bewildered.

"Please. Don't go."

I'm not ready for this to end. I take a seat in one of the two antique accent chairs in our living room, gesturing for him to sit in the opposite chair. That way we can be less than a foot away from each other but have distance too. He shakes his shoulders, huffs, and then sits down, clearing his throat before he speaks.

"So, you're a soul possessor?"

"Yes."

"What's that like? How did you?"

"It's a lonely way of being. As far back as I can remember, I haven't been able to hug anyone. An early memory I have of possessing a soul was at the Elementary School playground, but Timothy and I hit our heads on the slide we'd been under so the teachers chalked it up to mild concussion."

"Oh." He runs a hand through his hair.

There's a pause before he continues.

"Why didn't you tell me before?"

"It's complicated. I didn't want to lose you. I was afraid you wouldn't want to be around me anymore."

Boomer comes up to him and sets his head on Dave's knee as if he knows the man needs consoling. I pet Boomer and ponder. How come it had been so good at first? I've never been able to converse with someone like that. What caused it to change? When was the veil pierced? Did I alter the process somehow?

"Can I try something?"

He gulps.

"I promise to pull away if it's unsettling in the slightest."

"Okay." He doesn't seem completely mollified.

I put my hand on his, holding it the way I've dreamt of for so many years. He turns his hand up and squeezes mine. The smile on his face brightens the whole room. I'm in his thoughts, and he's in mine, but both are blissfully positive. I squeeze his hand back and then pull away before anything can go wrong, grateful to not feel any searing pain, the usual possession aftermath, in my head.

"That was…" I exclaim.

"I know…"

"Dave, can I ask? What's been upsetting you lately?"

"Ah, well, work's been a beast and…."

Molly walks in through the front door, interrupting us. Her eyes dart around, and her right hand is clenched into a fist in front of her chest. She seems spooked.

"Are you okay?"

Dave stands and approaches her, moving his head to investigate if she's all right. She seems to be frozen in a state of shock. I want to ask her if she hears ringing, but Dave's here, and I've already unloaded a lot on him tonight as it is, even that was breaking the rules.

It seems to click to her all of a sudden that she's safe at home. "I'm fine."

Dave puts a hand on her shoulder, bending his knees so he can look her in the eyes. "You sure?"

"Yeah."

"No one tried anything?"

"No, I was just spooked. Guess the dead body and…" she pauses and looks up before continuing, "everything has me on edge."

"Hm, I'm going to check the perimeter before I head home."

Really, he's heading home? Maybe all the soul possessing tired him out. It is nice that he's making sure everything's okay for Molly, but I wonder if he's dodging the question about what's been upsetting him lately.

"Be careful," I say to him.

"I will." He hugs me quick and then turns to go.

With that, Molly's zapped out of her stupor. Her eyes go wide. As soon as he's outside, she pounces on me with questions.

"Did Dave just hug you, Orla?"

My cheeks burn. "Yes." I can't hold back my smile.

"Oh...My...God!"

"I know"

"Tell me everything!"

"You go first. Did Cormac explain why she couldn't even text back?"

"Well..."

"Molly!"

"We were a little too preoccupied for talking."

"Mol-ly!"

She smiles, and I'm grateful that she was able to have a moment, but it's a guarded joy. When will Cormac ghost her next? I smile back, but it's not full. I don't want to see my friend hurt again.

All too quickly, her expression falls into one of concern.

"What is it?"

"I tried to warn her that I think she may be in danger."

"And?"

"She left. No explanation, just an awkward moment, denial, and then gone."

An "I told you so" is the last thing my friend needs right now.

"I'm sorry, Molly."

"It's okay. Now, your turn."

"We did more than hug, and oh my goodness, it was amazing. We visualized kissing each other and then kissed each other for real. He was such a natural in the beginning, at least. It was like his soul's been possessed before, like a million times, and he's practiced how to handle it."

"I'm thrilled for you. Told you not to wait so long."

"Thanks, but it didn't last."

"Oh?"

"Yeah, after a while, his secrets started flooding forward, and he couldn't handle it. Thoughts of aggression popped up."

"Not exactly the easiest thing to tackle. Maybe give him some time to get comfortable with that one."

"I have noticed his anger increasing lately. When Russ accidentally bumped into me at the bar, I thought Dave might punch him. His jaw clenched with fury at the mere sight of Oliver."

"Can't really blame him for that one."

"This is serious. I think it's getting further out of his control."

"Okay. So he has super soul possessing chill skills, at least for a bit of time but struggles to control his temper. He's not violent."

Dave pops his head back in the front door. "Coast is clear."

"Thanks, Dave."

I can see Molly pondering something.

"Hey, so you know about Orla, now."

Oh no, where's she going with this?

"Yeah, do you?" He pauses before answering his own question. "Of course." He moves his head from side to side.

"Well, just to let you in, she's not the only…." She can't be serious.

I jump in before she can continue, "It was good to see you."

But Dave's not letting it go. We're not supposed to share what we are. I've already broken the rules by telling him I'm a soul possessor, and now Molly's going to amplify that mistake by telling him she's half banshee. Great! "Come on, Orla," Molly complains.

"Fine, but I need to take Boomer for a walk. You guys talk about whatever." I'm pissed. I don't know what to do. They should know that I don't want this to happen now. Why is my best friend insisting on pursuing it? I glare at Molly, grab Boomer's leash, and then clip it on his collar. We head out the door with Dave and Molly staring after us in astonishment. Do they try to stop me? No.

Walking has a cleansing effect, no matter how upset I am. Usually, the emotion fades away as I take in my surroundings. But I'm not there yet. Dave knows I'm a soul possessor. If Molly continues the conversation she started, he'll also know she's a banshee. Will he ever look at us the same? His words ring through my head, "You never believe in anything supernatural." Now he'll know just how far from the truth that statement was.

But, more importantly than that, what we should have been paying attention to all along. There's a killer on the loose in our quaint village, and someone needs to find them. Something else has entered our town.

Something else with power. I feel it like goosebumps on the back of my neck.

*****

Walking along the sidewalk at night gives the town of Ethel a new look. Streetlamps and the moonlight provide enough glow to add shadows. The wind blows through a batch of trees and the branch shadows look like old, skinny, arthritis-riddled fingers reaching for me from the pavement. I follow my familiar path and soon come to iron gates complete with strategically placed metal vines. It's after hours, but that's never stopped me before. I enter and find my usual bench near the smaller gravestones and the lone firepit. There's firewood and dry kindling already set up. I light it and use a fire poker to move things around and allow the flame to build. Lying back on the bench, staring up at the stars, I can pretend I'm across the ocean, on a land I've never been to. This is the place I allow myself to connect with a thousand souls who have looked at the sky. I imagine I'm someone stronger who lets my magic be free and unhindered. For a second, I pretend I'm fully accepted that way. Just for one millisecond, everything can be fine.

Clouds block my view of the stars reminding me we have bigger obstacles right now. Who was the body? Anyone could wear jeans and a green shirt. I dig deeper into my memory. There'd been a hat and waterproof boots nearby. No one around here is rich enough to be murdered for their money... not that any amount of money is worth it. Sure we've had our disagreements and even scuffles now and then, but I can't fathom any of them progressing to murder. Lover's quarrels are often overheard or expected and called in or watched. The kinds of crime we tend to see is teenage vandalism. They're just at that age where anyone grapples with how to communicate the ferocious hormones and emotions raging in oneself. And we also have some minor theft and burglary, but it's usually individuals that are so famished, forgiveness and assistance are often ordered over charges and penalties.

I wonder if the detective has any leads. Would my asking cause them to suspect me? I should go visit Kyle. I'm sure he's picked up some gossip by now. Deciphering what to believe can be the hard part, but after living here so long, I think I've got the hang of it. I sit up and brush off my jacket and hair. A branch cracks to my right and behind me as if a boot stepped on it. Boomer growls. My breath freezes, and I reach for the poker, the tip still hot from sitting in the firepit. I hear another crunch as if leaves were stepped on this time instead of a branch and move to place the firepit between myself and whatever's approaching. Boomer's at my heels, ready to pounce, but I have ahold of his leash in my other hand.

I spot movement and follow it with my eyes. There's not much to make out but then I see the firelight glint off long, blonde hair. Boomer barks.

"Hey, who are you?"

"Orla?"

"Cormac?" No wonder I couldn't make out much. She's in all black, like usual.

"I thought I'd find you here."

"What are you doing?"

"Do you mind if I join you?"

"No." I point to the bench next to mine. "Boomer, quiet."

I return to my bench as she takes the one to my right.

"What'd you do to Molly? She came home all spooked."

"She's the one who spooked me. Kept talking about how she's seeing visions of me dying."

That actually makes sense, but I don't want to give her the satisfaction. She is the one who ghosted my best friend, after all. "Why are you looking for me?"

"You seem to be a bit more accepting of the supernatural than others."

She's saying this right after disclosing that she ended a conversation with Molly

66

because it was about visions. How does she not see how hypocritical she's being? "Okay."

"I need to put together a séance."

"Why?"

"I want to find out who the body was."

Okay, I'll have to give it to her. She's piqued my interest.

"What do you need from me?"

"Sitting around this fire is perfect." She pulls an incense stick, and board out of the black satchel slung over her shoulder. Then she tilts the stick into the fire until it lights and sets it on the board on the bench next to her. When she pulls the exact same hat I'd just seen in my memory out of her satchel, I gasp.

"Where'd you get that?"

She shrugs her shoulders. "We need it."

She sets the hat between the incense and the fire and then reaches her hands out to me.

"Can we do it without holding hands?"

"Wow, I knew you were protective of Molly, but I didn't know you detested me."

I huff. "I just have an aversion to touch." If she only knew just how much weight one carries with real power.

"Fine."

She uses her hands to sit crossed-legged, then places them in her lap and begins to chant an incantation.

"I to the waves lift mine eyes, from whence doth come my harmony...."

I zone out a little, which is probably not what I should be doing now, but then questions pull out of me as if I were a ventriloquist's doll. "Who are you?"

The flames flicker as a breeze rolls through, and with it, I swear I hear, "I'm a bohemian friend."

I look at Cormac. "Friend?"

She nods yes, and moves her hand in a circle as if to coax me to continue.

"What happened?"

The wind is stronger this time, blowing both of our hair into our faces. Somehow

68

there seems to be a bubble of protection around the hat and incense as they barely move. The wind picks up and is ferocious around us. A branch cracks, splits, and then falls onto the unoccupied bench. I suck in a breath. That had been close. An eerie prickling feeling oozes its way up my arms, but Cormac is waving her hand in a circle again.

"Is there still danger?"

Now we barely stand because the gust is so strong. Laced within it is the word: "Drogheda."

What in the actual fuck? "That's it!" I stand, and the wind stills.

"Wait. Thank you, Spirit. Please be at peace." Cormac quickly recites and then stands to follow me.

"Why? I'm done."

"Do you know what friend it could be?"

"No clue."

"Hey, I thought we were working together."

"That last word…Drogheda. It's what Molly hears every time she has a vision of you in danger."

She stops.

"Believe her now?" Boomer and I storm away without her answer.

CHAPTER SIX—MOLLY
"To learn one must be humble. But life is the great teacher."
James Joyce

"Maybe we shouldn't talk about it," Dave says. "Orla seems pretty upset."

"That's just because she has obvious reservations. I'm sure you of all people can understand how much she's been treated like the town recluse since she never touches anyone."

"Yeah."

"I mean, since it's a secret, the few people she has touched by accident never understood what occurred except that it was weird and anything but ordinary. It has just increased the mystery and stirred more rumors than anything. I think it would be better for her to be open about it."

"Is she allowed to do that? What about soul possessor code?"

"Have you ever met another soul possessor? What code? By keeping it a secret, she takes away the opportunity for those who would accept her to do so."

They've never fully accepted us, so I don't think we should abide by all their rules. Orla and Dave belong together; damn the magical society.

"Okay, I see what you mean. You know her as well, if not better than I do."

"And I understand her too because there's also something about me in which I keep a secret."

"What are you?"

"Don't ask it like I'm a pariah!"

"I'm not. Sorry, I was just wondering."

"It's okay. I shouldn't have snapped. How familiar are you with Irish folklore?"

"Hello, I'm an Ethel citizen too."

"Okay, okay, then, so you know what a ban…."

Every possible point in our house that has ever creaked lets out noise as if the entire house is being squeezed. Then wind whips all around us. I look at Dave, and first, his face is one of terror, all big eyes and stuff, but then it quickly turns to the one of anger we're beginning to get used to, eyebrows scrunched. The wind is strong enough it carries us up the stairs. I'm in such a shock that I don't want to believe what's happening, but I can't deny that Dave and I are floating. I pinch my arm to be sure I'm awake. There's pain, but it doesn't override the terror creeping up my skin like spiders. Dave grabs onto a spindle from the staircase railing, but it breaks off into his hands and is carried right along with us until he drops it in frustration.

When we approach a corner, I grab onto it with one hand and grab his hand with the other. The wind has our bodies lifted in the air. My hand on the wall our only point of contact. It's as if a hurricane is ripping through Ethel again, but instead, it's now just in the house. That's when I find the source. The concealed door at the end of the hallway is open!

My heartbeat flutters in terror. I want to scream, but the knot in my throat won't let me. I lose my grip as the wind picks up. Dave too, has spotted the source of the wind and places himself in front of me as if his body will block it, which works for some time. Eventually, though, the force is strong enough to make him collapse in on himself, balling up with his knees to his chest. My body follows in through the concealed door right after him. Once we're inside, the door slams shut, and the wind is gone. It smells like the bar when the local rugby team comes in after a game. Body odor reeks like someone camped in here for months without bathing.

I look around to take in our surroundings, but it's pitch black, and I can't see a thing. I feel warmth in my hand like someone's holding it, but there's nothing of substance there. I freeze.

"Dave?"

"Yeah, I'm over here. You okay?"

The wind picks up again. I say, "yes," but I can barely hear myself and I definitely don't hear an answer from him if he gives one. Then we're being moved once more. This time I feel the warmth without substance like before. It drags me to another point in this room or whatever it is we're in. I'm moved to a sitting position on the floor with my legs straight forward in front of me. Next, I feel warmth with substance against my back. Dave has been dragged to sitting with his back up against mine.

My hands are forced behind me, knuckles dragging on the wood floor, scraping cuts into my skin. My heart hammers in my chest. The adrenaline causes my breathing to quicken to an uneven pace. Rope rubs against our wrists binding them together. As soon as they're secure, we hear a snicker that echoes and then disappears. My nerves are frayed beyond imagination. My body shakes like a rickety old water tower ladder with a few loose screws.

"Little shithead," Dave says to the voice.

"Please don't piss it off," I rasp out between breaths.

"What was that?"

"I don't know." I can't say more because I'm almost in convulsions from the adrenaline surge in my body. I can tell Dave's trying to get his breathing back in check too. Right now, it's hard and heavy.

Orla warned us, but she knows it's difficult for me to listen for more reasons than one. Twisting my hands, I feel the rope burn against my skin. Dave's hands try removing our binding too. He really does love Orla. Sure, maybe he has a temper issue, but at least he's always stuck around. Which is more than I can say for any of my partners or anyone in my life. Except for Orla. She's been my rock. And yet here I am in a bind because I refused to listen to her.

The wind kicked in just as I was about to say the word "Banshee." That must be what triggered it. I don't understand why though. How would Dave knowing be harmful? Another reason why the ropes have me frayed is because they remind me of the visions with Cormac bound. Were the visions wrong? Or is Cormac also in a similar situation? How would my disclosing to Dave that I'm a banshee have anything to do with the visions? This is when I remember the Irish castle and the couple lost at sea. Were they not lost at sea but instead drug to a hidden spot by wind or a ghost or whatever that thing is? Perhaps the rumors of the banshee haunting the house were actually the couple screaming through gags for their lives. A shudder runs through me at the thought.

"Want to try to stand together?" Dave asks, pulling me out of my spiraling contemplations.

"Sure, why not, but I'm definitely not as tall as you so you might have to hunch down."

We bend our legs and push against each other's backs. I am not in the greatest shape, but my fear of Dave collapsing on me and being stuck here forever pushes me. We're a foot off the ground. Maybe we can do it. Another foot and the muscle strain is able to decrease. And then, we both bonk our heads on something and topple down onto our sides.

"Are you okay?" Dave asks. I think he's worried his large frame squashed mine, but there's not really much he could have done about it.

"Yeah, just a couple bruises."

"I'm sorry."

"You are not the one who put us in this situation."

"Yeah, I'm going to kill whatever did this to us."

"Simmer down."

"Really, in this circumstance."

"Okay, okay."

"Hey, can you reach my pocket? There should be something that can cut the rope there."

"Yeah." I feel the pocket clip from his knife before he utters another word and extract it. "I can cut the rope, but I'm doing it blindly." I open it up grateful for my years of service in the restaurant industry that have granted me dexterous hands.

"This rope is pretty thick. We can take turns if your hand tires out. I'd prefer that over the knife being dropped."

"Got it." I search for the rough part with my fingers. Then I angle it against the rope, so it won't cut either one of us. I begin rubbing the serrated section on the rope. With the angle of my hands, I'm only able to go up an inch and down an inch. This is going to take forever, but I can feel it making progress as a couple fibers break. After what seems like a million years but has probably only been a couple of minutes, Dave takes over. I can tell he's had much more practice with the knife. He's about halfway through when I take it back. Another round, and we're free.

"Yes!" I rub my sore wrists and check the bruised parts of my body.

"That's better." It sounds like Dave's rolling his shoulders or something.

We feel around the space, trying to find the door. Dave calls over to me when he locates a rectangular imprint that might be it.

"Damn it." He's trying to pull and push but not having any luck.

"There has to be a hinge or lock somewhere. We can use your knife once we locate it."

We search and search and search but are unable to find anything. He lets out an exasperated breath. So do I.

"Orla should get home before too long. She can help us," he says.

"You're right." But I really don't want to spend another second in here.

"I know you were going to share something, but let's not try repeating it otherwise, it might call back the wind."

"Agreed. Thank you. Even if Orla's no longer upset about that, I have to ask her to do something that will upset her."

"Oh?"

"Yeah, I want her to possess Cormac's soul so that I can find out what's going on with Oliver."

"Molly!"

"I know, I know, but desperate times call for desperate measures."

"So, she'll have to touch Cormac. Won't that give her secret away?"

"Yes, and no. Orla's become pretty good at smoothing the experience over so that if someone accidentally touches her, it's not too discomforting."

"Is that why I was able to touch her?"

"No, you have some like talented will against her power. It's as if you have a shield for a bit... might not last long now but perhaps with some practice."

"Yeah?"

"In fact, I'm going to want to look further into that later."

"Okay?"

"But, yes, it would be a lot of work for Orla. I just know that Cormac's in danger."

"She's not the only one."

True, we're the ones stuck.

"Do you think Cormac's in danger because she's hanging out with Oliver?"

"That's part of it."

"Even though I've known the guy for years, I've been getting a bad vibe off him lately."

Then there's scratching at the door, which has me on edge until I hear the accompanying bark.

"Boomer!"

"Good dog."

"That means Orla's back," I tell Dave.

"Maybe she can open the door from the outside."

"Orla, help," I yell. "I don't know. We haven't been able to before."

Hearing Orla's voice on the other side of the door almost brings tears of joy to my eyes.

"Molly? Dave? How'd you guys get in here?"

"It's a long story," I say.

"We're stuck," Dave adds.

"Hold on."

I hear her footsteps walk away. We had searched for how to open this door when we first moved in. We knew there was open space here from the layout of everything. We found the door by knocking on the wall until a hollow sound came back, but it was still concealed.

"Screw it."

"Orla?" I ask.

The sound of a drill has me smiling. Demolition Orla's the best.

"Yes!" Dave concurs.

She drills holes in the shape of an X and then hammers at it until there's a hole large enough for her fist to fit through. First, she hands over a pry bar and then another hammer.

"Dave, you take the west side of the door or frame. Whatever you can get to."

"You got the east?"

"Of course."

As I watch them now that there's some light in here, all I can think is how great of a team they make. They're obliterating our wall, and I couldn't be happier. They truly are meant for one another. Though I'm content to be free, a wariness creeps in as I consider the possibilities of this spirit. If it could suck Dave and I into a room, what could it possibly be doing to Cormac right now?

CHAPTER SEVEN – ORLA

"Come little children, I'll take thee away, into a land of Enchantment. Come little children, the time's come to play, here in my garden of magic." Sarah Sanderson, Hocus Pocus

"How in the world did you guys get in there?"

Dave struggles to climb out of the little entrance while Molly impatiently waits.

"It's a long story." She blows hair out of her eyes.

"When Molly began telling me what you didn't want her to, the house sucked us into that place." He points to the area behind the now broken door.

"You mean when she foisted information on you."

"Hey!" Molly looks insulted as she stretches her way into the hall through the opening.

"What's in there anyway?" I lean my head to get a view.

"It was too dark for us to see." Dave shrugs his shoulders.

"I'll go grab some flashlights." Molly runs off with Boomer following behind.

Dave brushes dust from his pants as I peek farther into the room to try to make out the dimensions. The ceiling's lower than the hallway ceiling. There's basic floorboard but no carpet or hardwood. The walls are also void of drywall finishing. The studs are viewable all around.

"Here." Molly hands us each a flashlight.

Neither one of them makes a move to enter the place they just escaped. I get it, but my curiosity wins. I start maneuvering my way in. A hint of a whisper seems to bounce along the walls around the room. It's weird, like nothing I've felt before, but I can tell there's a presence here.

A cold draft flows, and goosebumps prickle my arm. It's followed by the smell of rotten eggs. I move the flashlight around, taking in the room. Cobwebs and bits of insulation can be found as well as decades-old dust. There's a couple of paths along the floor that disrupt the dirt. Torn rope sits in the center. I spot the shape of something in the corner. Tiptoeing toward the small, rectangular object, I see pages within a tattered leather cover. The golden embossed cursive writing on the outside says: Daily Journal.

The diary looks about a century old. A warm draft blows from the opposite direction. I'd felt the cold draft. Must have to do with the fragile, antique house as well as its equally old heating and cooling system. The air causes the diary to open, pages fluttering in the wind. Then it stops leaving the journal's spine bent backward. The writing is so eloquent. I know this is probably private, but I'm drawn to it anyway. I read: *Don't worry. I know the signal. I can post it faster than Bob can finish a limerick.*

Before I can read further, a giggle sounds right behind me. I turn around to see what it is, but my flashlight goes out, and

I'm suddenly on the ground being pulled by something I cannot see. It feels like someone's touching me but I'm not possessing their soul. Three things hit me all at once: the pounding of my heart, gasping for air, and nauseousness. What in the hell is happening?

"Orla?" It sounds like Dave's not having an easy time reentering this place.

"Hurry up." Molly's impatient as ever, thank goodness.

Boomer's barking as if an intruder has entered our home. I tremble. The strange snicker bounces off the walls echoing back to me as my back rubs against the floor. "Dave!"

He drops to the ground upon entry, with Molly falling on top of him and Boomer not too far behind. They stumble to me while shining their flashlights, trying to find the being in our hidden room to no avail. Then Dave's holding me, actually holding me. With his arms around me, I grab onto his broad shoulders. His solid chest against me makes me feel safe as he carries me out of the room.

"Are you okay?"

The presence I had felt before disappears as quickly as it came. My heartbeat slows down and my breathing returns to normal. There is complete comfort being in his arms. It's as if he's pumping warm support to me through my connection to his soul. How is this happening? But I begin to sense worry trickling in, and much too soon, he's releasing me.

Boomer's in my lap next, licking my face, and I can't help but smile.

"We should have never let you go in there after what happened to us." Molly lets out an exasperated breath.

"Why, what happened to you in there?"

"It was awful." Dave runs his hand down his face.

"Yeah, something pulled us and tied our hands." Molly's pacing in our hallway.

"What was it?"

"I don't know." The way he looks at me is desperation personified.

I can tell they're both pretty shaken by the experience. Then Molly looks at me as if an idea just bloomed. "You could see what happened to us since we're not able to explain."

"What?" I ask.

"Just hold my hand." She reaches her hand out to me.

"Molly… you know what that will do…,"

"I know but I'd rather that than try to explain what we experienced."

"That bad, huh?"

"Really," Dave's looking down at Molly. "First, you're considering putting her through that with someone else and now with you?"

"What are you talking about?" I'm so confused.

"It's nothing." She looks like she could kill him. "Can we please just board this room back up?"

That does sound good to me. I already have the tool kit here. I look at Dave. "Can you grab a few of the boards from the shed?"

I turn to my roommate and give her *the look* after Dave has walked away.

"What?" she asks.

"He said you were considering me possessing someone else's soul before you suggested I possess yours."

"Oh, that."

"Yeah, that."

"Listen. I know something's going on with Cormac helping Oliver. I don't believe they're just communicating with ghosts. There's got to be more to it."

I hesitate. At first, I want to argue and say she's so wrapped up in the girl she's not thinking clearly. But then I remember the séance and Molly's visions. "Fine, I agree with you."

"Good…because this is important."

"Okay." I don't like the look on her face.

"There is something in that room. Dave and I both witnessed it, not to mention we were attacked by it, and it went after you. There's nothing else here that could do something like that. We think you can help with this next part because there may be some danger involved. Well, I think it has something to do with the haunting of Oliver's crew and my visions."

Whatever happened definitely spooked Molly. She doesn't usually ramble like this.

"What do you mean? How can I help?"

"I need to know exactly what Cormac is doing to help the crew."

"You already said that—so?"

"I need you to possess her soul."

"But you know what that will do to me."

"I wouldn't ask if I didn't believe it was of utmost importance."

"But how is that going to help you guys?"

"That's what I need to know. You can see and hear things when you're in someone else's soul, right?"

I'm not sure. "I've never tried reaching external sources while possessing a soul. I will be able to see her thoughts and memories, though."

Dave returns with the requested boards and looks at Molly like she's crazy. Then he points to me with a screwdriver in his hand. "You're actually going to ask her to do this?"

Molly steps closer to him and puts a hand on his arm. She growls, "Do you have a superior idea? Can you come up with anything better than my suggestion?"

He shakes his head no, but he doesn't look happy about it either. He throws the hammer down onto the floor. "You know what, fine. Do it. Never mind the years you couldn't touch me but all of a sudden, you will touch another person just because Molly asks you to."

93

The way he's looking at me makes me feel like I'm the one who's done something wrong. I really don't need this. What about our blossoming relationship?

"Dave, it's not like that. People are in danger," I plead, but he turns away. I hold my hand over his shoulder, wondering if it's safe to touch him, wanting to comfort him so badly. My hand rests on his shoulder for the quickest second. Eventually, he nods in agreement.

"Okay, but I wish you would have asked earlier, Molly. I was just with Cormac at the graveyard."

"Desperate times call for desperate measures," Molly says. "Wait, you were with Cormac?"

First, shock hits her face. Then she recovers and looks back at me with pleading eyes that say do this for me...please?

"How do you suggest I do this? I'm guessing you don't want her to know that it's happening."

"Well." Molly has her evil planning look plastered on her face as Dave secures the boards up, closing off the haunted room. "The Ethel Festival of Samhain is coming up."

"Plenty of distractions and time," Dave finally agrees, seeming to end his bickering.

"You want to possess her soul at the Celtic Festival?" I ask. Instantly I think of the bonfire and how the Ethel citizens will bring offerings to toss into the pyre. Everyone will be in costume, and the kids will bob for apples. We'll have every candle lit by midnight when the local musicians walk the streets serenading the town in a tradition thought to cleanse us each year.

Molly nods. "She's not going to be expecting it."

I start to speak but then shut my mouth when I realize that I'm standing next to a haunted room while considering doing this. Possess her soul? What if it doesn't work because something goes wrong? If Dave has to resort to punching Oliver, he will. Possessing souls on purpose is punishable by my kind, but I haven't exactly told anyone else that, not even Molly though I think she knows. And now we're talking about doing it on someone who may or may not know what she's doing and not even telling her how dangerous the consequences could be for us all. Molly swallows hard and stares me down like she can make me comply through sheer force.

Another downfall to this plan is the Festival of Samhain itself. During this time, my ability is heightened, yes, but that's because it's also when dead souls revisit loved ones. Which means I'll be constantly surrounded by them, making it harder for me to control the possession of another. Possessing the dead is not my favorite part of this gift. Possession of the living isn't either, but I've found workarounds, and I luckily can only do it to one other person at a time. Dave seems to be the best at being able to work with me in tandem during the process. I'm not exactly sure why that is, but I've never experienced this kind of control from another soul before.

Possession is a gift that requires immense concentration to control. Possession of the living is like getting tangled in a web of thoughts and emotions, especially when you're close to them. Possession of the dead can also be overwhelming, but not having the soul fight against me while I search for answers has lessened my headache. Possessing another person usually leaves me with splitting headaches and dizziness afterward. Sometimes it's worse than others, depending on how much I exert myself and how long I'm able to maintain possession each time I do it. And yet, I can't think of another way we're going to get the complete story from Oliver and Cormac.

I'm done arguing so I cross my arms over my chest and shrug at Molly after she sighs her relief at my submission. "Let's get this over with."

CHAPTER EIGHT – MOLLY

"The new white yacht with tall slender masts restlessly awaited her departure. Above the din of bustle and confusion rose high pitched and excited voices. Groups of people stood on the dock and stared, while others were tangled in last minute embraces."
Cruise of the Norther Light, Borden

I can't believe Orla has agreed to possess Cormac's soul. I'll finally get to know exactly what she's been up to out at sea. I take a deep breath while watching my roommate, fearing she'll change her mind. "We have some time to plan out the logistics. Dave and I can be close to ensure nothing bad will happen."

Boomer looks at the boarded-up door and whines. His tail's between his legs, and his hackles are raised.

"How about we plan somewhere else? This place gives me the creeps now." Dave's pacing back and forth stealing glances at the haunted room as if he's guarding us from it.

"Yeah, I'm not really sure I could fall asleep knowing that presence is down the hall," Orla says.

"You could stay at my place," Dave offers, and my heart melts watching them. He's loved Orla for so long.

"Yeah, you should stay with Dave, Orla." I nod. "I can stay with Cormac."

"Will you be able to refrain from spilling the beans?" Orla knows me too well.

"For this, I can."

"Okay." She tilts her head to the side, and I can't tell if she's impressed or pondering something.

"I can ensure she'll be at the festival by inviting her to go with me. That way, I can be privy to important details too."

"That's a great idea." Dave's eyes get bigger when he thinks something's a good idea.

Orla puts her arm around his shoulders. I'm filled with relief that she's finally able

99

to touch another person. "Why don't you help me pack?"

They leave, and I turn to go to my room to do the same. My skin tingles thinking of the bath Cormac and I might share once I'm at her place. Hers is large enough to fit two easily, one of those jacuzzi things.

*****

Letting myself into Cormac's apartment brings back so many memories. When she nursed me after a hangover with electrolytes and greasy food. I look at the double-sided easel in the center of the living room where we've spent so many hours. She's into realism and her portraits are the most life-like that I've seen. She helped me find my love of the abstract though she's never known the reason it called to me, a way to express what the effects of the ringing did to me. Of course, the last time we were here, I told her about my visions, and she ran off. I hope we can just make up. Her being mad at me is the worst.

When I turn around, she's there. Cormac steps forward, and my stomach flips like I'm riding a roller coaster. I nod and grin at her, hoping it will win her over.

"Look what the cat dragged in."

"Hey!" I playfully jab her in the arm.

"You finally come to terms with my independence?"

"Like I could stop you from hanging out with Oliver if I wanted to?"

"Exactly, you should know better by now."

"Guess I'll have to distract you for as long as I can instead."

I take a deep breath and try to slow my pounding heart as Cormac moves closer toward me across the room, her eyes studying mine for any sign of fear like they used to hold when we first met. She doesn't need to know that fear has become incidental now that I'm used to her presence. No matter what I've been through, her energy is calming instead of intimidating or frightening since I know her better than strangers ever

101

would. I feel as if we've been connected for an eternity.

Cormac's lips meet mine again, and this time, they're forceful and demanding. She plunders my mouth hungrily and suddenly, we're kissing like there's no tomorrow: hot, hard, and fast until Cormac pushes me against the wall so strongly it hurts but feels so good. Her hands are all over me, her mouth covering my neck in kisses that make me shiver. Cormac pulls away from the kiss to murmur, "I can't stop thinking about you" in my ear. She groans and starts kissing me again before I have the chance to respond. Cormac grabs my hips and presses her body against mine so tightly it feels sublime. She's touching me everywhere at once.

The warmth of Cormac's breath against my ear makes me gasp with need as she whispers, "I've got something for you." Before I know what's happened, Cormac grabbed my waist and lifted me up so she can carry me to her room and lay me down on the bed. Cormac's hovering over me with her lips brushing against mine. Cormac kisses my neck softly as her hands run from my hips to the hem of my shirt, making me gasp as her fingertips brush across my skin, leaving a trail of goosebumps in their wake as Cormac slowly pulls my shirt off and tosses it away. I rip her shirt off, too, and groan at how gorgeous she is. As we both become undressed, this feels more right than anything ever has before.

Cormac's hands start to explore my body, touching me all over. She captures my mouth and her warm tongue is on mine again, even more passionately than only moments ago. Her hands move over my lower stomach and down the side of my leg until her fingertips brush up against my inner thigh, making me suck in air in surprise at how sensitive her touch is when she nudges closer into my arms, then places one hand up my side while the other slowly moves around my thighs stroking my skin with each pass of her hand as it progressively gets higher and higher.

I groan in pleasure when she presses our bodies together then she does it again, making me moan into her mouth. We both gasp with pleasure as our bare skin brushes against each other when our pelvises mold together so closely that I can feel desire digging into my stomach, making me squirm at how good it feels to be pressed together like this.

"Want to take a bath?" I ask.

"You are the queen of interruption."

"What? I thought you liked it."

"We were kind of in the middle of something."

"And we can continue. Come on." I roll us to our sides and sit up. Then I grab her hand and begin guiding her to the bathroom. I wrap her cotton robe around her and place a folded towel on the bath step. As the water runs, I massage her shoulders. "Hang on." I kiss her forehead and then run to my backpack. Grabbing the candles, bath bubbles, and incense, I imagine Cormac's glorious smile.

She rubs my shoulders as I set everything up, and before too long, the bath is ready, the lighting is a warm glow, and it smells of heaven in the bathroom. Cormac steps in, her foot pointed like a ballerina.

Then her naked body is half submerged in bubbles.

"I feel like I should be saying, 'get your ass in here,' but that doesn't seem very proper." She smiles as she pats the empty space next to her.

"You are so bad. But you won't hear me complaining." I join her in the tub and snuggle up next to her while she turns off the tap with a flick of her finger before laying back against my chest.

"This feels good," she murmurs happily, then kisses me on the cheek.

"Oh, it does? May I?" She nods yes. I kiss her neck softly, then wrap my arms around her waist, pulling us closer until we're touching everywhere again. I slip my hand between her legs while holding her chin up and continuing to kiss her neck. I navigate to the area of most pleasure between her legs with my hand while moving my other hand to her nipple. She arches her back in satisfaction and then lowers it in a repetitive motion that causes ripples and waves in the water. I pinch and pull her nipples, moving back and forth while flexing my other wrist in penetration over and over. I continue to massage my fingers against her as she pushes her pelvis against my palm. Our breathing intensifies until it's ragged, and she explodes in ecstasy.

As soon as we've recovered our breath, she moves to the other side of the bath and sits down while pulling me onto her lap so I'm straddling her as we kiss. She runs her hands up my back as our lips touch again. Her nails gently scratch down my back, and I softly tug her hair. As the kiss continues, her hands find their way to my body. My nipples harden with the touch of her tongue, and she sucks on them in return. I push against her palm as my breathing becomes ragged. While her finger massages in a perfect pattern, the thumb is what I'm most interested in. It massages at my most sensual part. I cradle my head on her shoulder as I pant and pant and pant.

Suddenly Cormac stands up with me in her arms and steps out of the tub, still holding me close to her body. She says, "Shut your eyes." I oblige.

She sets me down, and as I stand, I hear things moving around. The anticipation is painful, waiting, waiting, and waiting some more. Then she picks me back up and moves me again. Laying me down naked. "Okay, open."

When I open my eyes, I see that we're now lying on her bed. It's been covered with towels on top of the bedsheet because it's covered in water since we just got out of the tub. Cormac's putting lotion on my skin right now, making me groan at how sensitive I am after the bath. Her hand goes up my leg slowly on the outside of my thighs as her mouth travels on the inside of them. She expertly sucks and licks while my head buzzes. Despite the goosebumps covering my naked skin, I feel a radiating heat at my core. I scream out her name as she brings me to completion. We both lay on our backs, hands, and feet numb from our exertion.

I roll toward Cormac and rub my finger on her lip. "I love you."

She smiles, pulling a blanket over us, and then moves my hair behind my ear. "I love you too."

We curl up into one another, ready for sleep, but before we drift off, I have to get one question out. "Why are you helping Oliver so much?"

"You know I commune with the dead. That's what they need right now."

I rub my hand down her arm, tracing her tattoos. They're a mix of sunflowers and goth like Alice in Rockstar land instead of Wonderland. "Yeah, but surely he's not the only one."

She huffs. "Okay. I can never hide anything from you."

"Ah, so there is more to the story."

"Oliver lost his family in a heartbreaking disaster." She gulps. I can see her Adam's apple move up and down. "Like mine."

"I'm so sorry, Cormac. I don't mean to trudge up bad memories. But are you saying his family was burned to death like yours?"

Now she takes a deep inhale, turns toward the ceiling, and then exhales. "No, it's worse."

I sit up with that. "Worse than being burned alive?"

She shudders. "Yes, they were tortured for weeks; it was...awful."

"Damn, I never knew that. I mean, we don't get too many newcomers to Ethel, but the ones we do usually bring a story with them. I guess I never pushed to find out why he didn't."

"Yeah, that's why when you told me about the visions, I freaked out so bad."

"Wait, what? How are they connected?"

"His family was tied by ropes throughout the entire torture."

"But my visions are from long ago, not decades ago but centuries."

"Still, just the thought of being bound brings it back. I'm visited by nightmares over and over again."

I turn back to her and hold her. I want to comfort Cormac. Her head rests on my arm as I rub her back, tracing the tattoo there that I know by heart. I keep rubbing until her breathing becomes heavy, and I know she's asleep. Thinking about Cormac's and Oliver's shared tragedies makes me wonder how that binds them together. Do they think the ghosts might be their family members reaching out? They both could definitely use some closure. Why would multiple members of the crew have seen and heard the ghosts individually?

Something's not right. While I'm glad Cormac shared with me what she could, I still feel that the only way to get to the whole truth is through Orla possessing Cormac's soul and seeing what Cormac sees.

CHAPTER NINE – ORLA

"Sail forth—steer for the deep waters
only,
Reckless O soul, exploring, I with thee,
and thou with me,
For we are bound where mariner has not
yet dared to go,
And we will risk the ship, ourselves and
all."
Whitman

Driving to Dave's family farmhouse feels like traveling through time. The clouds are so low today that I swear I can see their reflection in the water, like a painter's version of heaven. As we near, I see the kayaks stored in a row. How many times have Dave and I used them; I can't recall. I think part of me spent so many hours here because of the familial feeling that had been lacking in my life. The pictures strategically hung along the stair wall give proof of how much family had taken root in the place throughout the years.

As soon as Dave parks the truck Boomer jumps out of the back to run up to Nessa, Dave's tan Labrador. I love seeing them play here where they're able to run about free on all of the land. Walking up the entry stairs, I take in the wrap-around porch recalling many nights swinging on the hanging porch swing over hot tea and music. The rustic aesthetic warms me to my bones as we enter the house. Dave takes my bag off my shoulder and sets it on the front entry bench. Since the touch is only a skim, I only feel a slight tickle, no possession.

"You hungry? I'm starved."

I follow him to the kitchen, noticing every sound. While this house used to be full it no longer is. Now it's a solitary place for Dave. Sadness threatens to overwhelm me.

"What do you have?"

He rustles through the fridge and pantry, grabbing steak, veggies, and rice.

"Does stir-fry sound good?"

"Perfect."

He preps the steak while I chop veggies.

"So Molly said I respond to your soul possession differently than others." He looks at me with curiosity in his eyes.

"Yeah, you seem to have more control over what I see and hear."

He nods and starts chopping the steak into small morsels tossing it in a pan to brown. I watch his arms move about with sureness in my body, knowing in some ways he is my home, and in others, he is not. Knowing that in the past, when we were together as friends, Dave led me toward many paths of discovery makes me happy to be by his side today once again. Especially now that we might actually be able to touch one another.

"You think she was speaking metaphorically?"

"No, you have real skill, but I'd like to see if we can make it last longer."

"How can we do that?"

"This might sound backward but when I touch you, try to send something specific forward. Eventually, once you have that down, you should be able to keep back certain things too."

"I have nothing to hide from you." His shoulders tense as he says this.

"Dave, we're going to have to work on the anger that's been bothering you lately, figure out the root source, but let's start with something easier."

He exhales, and his shoulders relax. "Okay." He smiles, and it takes control on my part not to melt right then and there.

"Do you have something simple and fun in mind to push forward?"

"Yeah."

When I touch him, we're automatically back in each other's minds. Quickly an image pushes forward. I'm hoping this is the image Dave had intended. It's from years back when we were teens. We had been racing in the kayaks, and I finally beat him by splashing water in his face and passing him. I can feel both of our stomachs ache because of how much we had laughed.

It had been one of the best days I can recall. When that image is clear, Dave closes his eyes, and he's pushing forward with me; more pictures flood my mind of us surfing, him setting a step up for me so I could climb onto a horse and we could ride around the property, him showing me how to make rosemary apple pie when we were young, learning how to find the best fishing and cockle digging spots. Our lives are full because of the time spent together. It's all so wonderful that it makes my heart ache seeing it all again. We worked well as partners then, just like now. This memory proves our ability to trust each other in ways that should never be surpassed. I know why we're such good friends, and I cherish it.

When I feel a hint of a trigger that might stir anger in Dave, I pull my hand away. His face is serene and peaceful, so I hope he didn't notice what I felt at the end.

Dave opens his eyes and smiles at me again. "We did so much together."

I nod, grateful that no headache seems to be on the horizon. We finish dinner and watch TV snuggled with pillows on the couch, just like old times. We're close together but not touching. Boomer and Nessa are curled up at our feet. We can practice his soul possession control more later. I can tell he's worn out from earlier. He falls asleep quickly after all that hard work, while I can't seem to doze off no matter how hard I try. I lower the television volume as he drifts off deeper into sleep. Trying not to wake him, I get up from the couch and slowly walk away to look out the window. A light is on in the barn out back. I feel as if I'm in some sort of daze.

My heart quickens as I head outside toward the light. Not sure what I'm expecting to find but almost certain Dave won't like it if he finds me checking things out by myself. The barn door creaks open and swings shut behind me as soon as I step inside.

Despite the darkness I just came from, my eyes adjust quickly, scanning for anything that might jump out at me. It looks like someone has been staying here. There are three full camping pots with canned food next to them on a foldout table. Panic runs through my veins.

Dave opens the door to the barn. "Hey, babe, what are you doing?" His voice is groggy with sleep, but he looks at me seriously trying to figure out my intentions by my facial expression. He walks toward me, reaching his hand out. A strange ping sound penetrates the empty space drawing both our attention.

Before I can warn Dave, there are three people in robes standing behind him pointing crossbows aimed right between his shoulders. My heart drops to my stomach. They're now chanting something that sounds like Latin, and Dave is staring at them dumbfounded, shaking his head up and down like he agrees with them. The hairs on the back of my neck rise. Behind them I see a familiar figure. Ben, Kyle's fiancé, is gagged and bound in rope. He should be safe at the museum or at the pub with Kyle. How did he get here? What do they want with him? My skin turns icy cold. Dave swings around, trying to catch all three robed intruders at once, but they're gone. Dave looks at me, confused and shocked that the men were even here in the first place.

"What happened?" Dave rubs his head, looking down toward the crossbows on the ground, "Did you see those guys? I thought I heard voices or something like chanting coming from out here." His brow wrinkles as he continues to look around, still rubbing his temples.

My forehead crumples too. "I think someone has been staying out here. There are canned goods on a table by the door. There were three people chanting something about a third soul and something about a sacrifice. Ben was tied up behind them, but I don't see him either now." I wave my hands in the air. "They aimed bows at you, then disappeared into thin air!"

Dave cracks his knuckles as he looks around again; clenching his fists, he says aloud like they could still be here to hear him, "Well, no one is sacrificing Ben or anyone else."

I jump, finding myself back on the couch. Boomer's snoring, and Dave's still asleep. Nessa's looking out the window from my dream or vision or whatever that was. I'm so relieved it wasn't real. She paces and then sits in front of me. "What was that, girl?" I whisper as I scratch behind her ear. First, Molly's having visions of Cormac being bound, then I'm seeing Ben captured. What was it that they said in my dream? Something about sacrifice that does not sound good at all. I've never had visions before; that's Molly's thing. I usually only see into others during a possession. Was it my proximity to Dave and his strange possession abilities? So many questions, so few answers.

Something about being so close to Dave, maybe it's a bond thing. I rub my head, trying to sort out how I can help Molly and Dave with this puzzle. "You okay, girl?" Nessa lays her head on my lap, licking my hand in comfort. Why has Ben become a target? He stands up for those who get bullied in town. Is someone tired of him being supportive and protective? Most of his actions are provoked. Whereas Kyle, on the other hand, tends to instigate tension by calling people out on being in the wrong. Did someone finally have enough? It doesn't make sense. I really do need to possess Cormac's soul. I just wish there were a better way.

Possessing another is punishable by my kind. Of course, I just broke that rule with Dave but I trust him to keep my secret. I would be possessing Cormac without consent, so I don't think she'd hesitate to turn me in. It would give her the leverage to be accepted by the supernatural society she's been looking for. Another thing that makes me leery of the festival is the secret gathering beforehand. While Molly and I might be the only supernatural residents of Ethel, there are many in the world. Every year they come to Ethel around this time for the gathering. What should make us feel accepted finally does the opposite. Even at the gathering, we're treated like outsiders because we're halflings. It's just another reminder that we're different.

Nessa shakes her head back and forth while watching the door. I look at Dave to find him already staring at me, "Who were they? Did you see it? Is that why you're up?" He pats the couch next to him, inviting me to sit closer.

I scoot onto the couch, "You saw it too. Three men in robes chanted something about sacrifice and a third soul. Then they aimed crossbows and disappeared into thin air! You saw all of that?"

Dave grabs my hand without flinching. "They took Ben? Was it real, or a vision of things to come?" He looks down at our hands entwined on his lap, and I see what the vision looked like to him.

I turn to face him, sitting crossed-legged while we're still holding hands. A memory of Dave's surfaces. He and Ben are at the museum laughing so hard that tears escape their eyes. Then, while continuing to touch Dave, my possession travels through to the person he's thinking of, Ben. Now, it's as if I were touching Ben and seeing his thoughts. Thoughts of planning the perfect wedding filter in, letting me know that he's okay.

"Dave!"

"Yeah?"

"I was able to possess Ben's soul through you!"

CHAPTER TEN – MOLLY

"I was born on the night of Samhain, when the barrier between the worlds is whisper-thin and when magic, old magic, sings its heady and sweet song to anyone who cares to hear it."

— Carolyn MacCullough, Once a Witch

I look over my shoulder while frying an egg in a skillet to see Cormac walk into the kitchen in only a t-shirt. Her hair's all askew, making her even more adorable than usual. I smile at her while she fills the coffee maker with water. Then she wraps her arms around me and kisses the back of my neck. Working late hours makes sleeping in a superb option.

"You seem happy this afternoon." She takes a seat at the small two-seater table in the kitchen.

"I'm nervous. I want to ask you something." I lift the egg and place it on a plate that already has bacon and a roll.

She has her chin in her hand and elbow on the table when I set the plate in front of her. "So, what is it?"

"Will you be my date to the Ethel Festival of Samhain?"

She has the audacity to actually smirk. Damn her. "I would love to."

I scarf down my food with only one pause. "We need to get ready soon?" My excitement is making my stomach sour with nerves, but this delicious food overrides it.

After we're dressed, she walks behind me, and wraps her arms around my waist pulling me against her chest. "If you don't start walking now, we will definitely be late for work." She kisses the side of my head on the spot that always makes me weak in the knees, then releases me laughing on our way out the door holding hands like giddy teenagers on their first date.

We walk into town hand-in-hand, finding Kyle at his usual spot behind the bar. "What'll it be?" he asks with a wink knowing we can't partake in any spirits before a shift.

I sit on a stool next to Cormac, and we both order coffee; then I notice the pile of pumpkins in the center of the bar.

"What are all these pumpkins for?" I ask while watching him move around behind the counter like a ninja preparing our drinks with ease and finesse.

"Tomorrow is Samhain so they put out extra decorations to get people into the mood." He winks at me again, "You know what that means?"

I shake my head, knowing he's about to tell me. "No, I don't. What does it mean?"

"It means you can cast spells on anyone or anything that pisses you off!" He laughs while placing our drinks on coasters, then snags his rag from under the bar and starts wiping down some spilt beer.

"Why would I ever want to do that?"

He takes a deep breath while cocking his head far back and closing his eyes. "You can make it rain on their wedding day…so long as it's not mine! Be creative like my favorite witches, Willow and Tara!" He laughs again with me joining him after a moment of being teased. Buffy the Vampire references always have a way of calming me down. "What about you, Cormac? Are you going to try anything fun with that magic of yours?"

She sips her coffee, then places it back on the coaster putting an elbow up on top of the bar, resting her chin in her hand again. "You know, I have heard there's a gathering of witches just before the festival."

How does she know about that? "Looks like the band is ready to warm up." I point to the stage.

"Guess it's time to clock in. Thank you for the coffee, Kyle."

"And your tables are filling up," Kyle tells me, letting me know I need to begin my shift too.

The bar's alive with a buzz. Everyone's discussing Samhain. I get to hear what costumes some of the regulars are planning to wear. I enjoy the laughter and companionship that I'm surrounded by. Hours tick by, and the sun sets.

The crowd suddenly becomes noisy with commotion coming from the parking lot. The singing stopped, and Cormac's heading toward the exit. The rest of the band continues in an attempt to keep the crowd calm.

"I'll be right back," Cormac says while placing her hand on my shoulder to reassure me she'll return soon.

Kyle is standing in front of me, processing whatever he's seeing from outside even though it looks like his face should say something other than what it does. He steps away for a moment then returns with different eyes. "There's fire on the island."

I don't hear ringing, so hopefully, that means all are okay... unless my power's somehow suddenly stopped. It was slow last time. "Is the fire chief aware of that?" I ask, wondering if it's too late to shelter Cormac from hearing about the fire.

He looks out toward the crowd then speaks with a voice of shock and concern. "I don't think the fire chief is here. Remember she had to travel out of town."

I stare at him for a long moment trying to figure out what he's not saying; now concerned with people's lives? The hair on the back of my neck raises in fright. What in the hell are we going to do? "Call anyway so the rest of the firefighters can get the fire boat prepped!"

The music's stopped and those of us inside have all gathered around a table where a customer has a scanner pulled up so we can hear the emergency messages and follow what's happening.

Shortly after the call, we hear the crew sending the boat to extinguish the fire. Everyone continues to listen until the last flame is reported to be extinguished, and then Kyle persuades everyone back to their seats.

"I think that might have had to do with the spirits that have been visiting Oliver's crew." Cormac's talking to a table toward the back. I notice her hands shaking but am at a loss as to why she's mentioning him again.

This I have to hear. "Oliver?" Oliver Oliver Oliver Oliver Oliver, I think.

"Well, Oliver's been seeing ghosts since the turn of the season." She pivots toward me. "I've been helping him communicate to them, as you know. Lately, the ghosts have been talking about destruction so when the island goes up in flames, more than likely it could have something to do with a spirit or ghost."

I tear my eyes away from her and turn to the window watching the rest of the crowd disperse. It sounds like all of the volunteer firefighters have gone that way, and no one was hurt. I'm hopeful for our plans for tomorrow night on Samhain, but that quickly deflates when Oliver enters the bar.

He makes his way through the crowd until he reaches us near the back of the pub. "I need to talk to you." Oliver points at Cormac then me while trying not to raise his voice. "Both of you," he adds when neither of us moves from our places.

"We're all ears, Oliver," I tell him, playing along.

Oliver motions for us to step away, and we do so and head toward what's known as 'Kyle's office'. It's a small dark room containing an old desk and some chairs used for storing extra glasses and other dishes out of sight but easily accessible in case we have any large events or parties without enough seating in the dining area.

Oliver closes the door behind us and sits in one of the chairs. "I just heard about what happened to the island." Oliver speaks with a sense of calmness, but I can see it's an act. His eyes are desperately searching for secrets. "Do you know anything about it?" he asks Cormac, who quickly turns toward me, looking like someone has slapped her across the face.

"What secrets do you want, Oliver?" she says to him. "I'm your friend, not your messenger lady."

"Then what message did they give you that there was destruction coming? That could have been me, Cormac; my house is on that island!" Oliver yells out, pointing to his chest and then at Cormac.

"That is the message, Oliver," she says in a calmer voice.

"Doesn't that piss you off?" Oliver asks me, accusatory sounding. "I know for a fact it would have pissed me off. Her hiding so much."

I know that Cormac would be mad if I go easy on her because of her family so I follow Oliver's direction, but I'm ready to embrace or run after the woman I love if it seems she needs that instead…actually, I wish she did… "It does, but I'm not going to make a scene about it." I pause and then address Cormac instead of Oliver. "I want to hear it all too."

"Fine, fine, jeez." I can tell Cormac wants to pace but there's no room for that. "You know how they mentioned something about not having papers?"

"Yeah, I remember that." Oliver rubs the back of his neck.

"Well, they've also been talking about how an attack of an island off a port would be most advantageous."

"I thought you mentioned torture instead of a fire before," I can't help but raise my voice a little.

"I was hoping to have it all figured out before worrying anyone. You see," she takes a breath, "something clicked when you told me about your visions."

"This has to do with my visions too?"

She nods. "I've just noticed some similarities, what with this being an Irish town. We're a port, smaller, near a larger one, Salem. Ireland has two such ports. A large one being Belfast and a smaller one named Drogheda."

It feels like the air has been knocked out of me. "What does this mean?"

"Well, I've done some research on Drogheda. Have you ever heard about the siege that took place there?"

It feels as if a fist grips my heart when I hear the name Drogheda.

"Oh yeah, the Cromwellian conquest." Oliver lights up.

"You know about it?" I ask while rubbing my chest.

"It was awful." Cormac looks pretty distraught. "Not only did the military attack and win but they kept on killing even after the battle was over. They didn't stop with those who had fought against them but everyone in town."

I think back to the visions of Cormac being bound, ready for execution. I also remember the dead body discovered in town recently. Something is definitely going on.

"Are the ghosts trying to warn us or is it more like a premonition?"

"I was hoping to figure that out before telling you."

I pull her into my arms. "But now we can figure it out together."

Oliver opens the door. "I need to tell the crew."

CHAPTER ELEVEN – ORLA

"May the road rise up to meet you, may
the wind be always at your back, may the
sunshine warm upon your face…"
— An Irish Blessing

"You what?" Dave asks.

"I possessed Ben's soul just by touching
you while you were thinking about him.
I've never been able to do that before."

"What does that mean?"

"I need to ask someone with more experience." Luckily, there will be plenty
with more experience here soon.

"Is he okay?"

"He seemed to be okay, at least for now.
I just saw him in the museum like usual."

"Well, that's good." Dave fluffs the pillows on the couch between us and gives me
a sheepish grin. It probably would be best
if we went back to sleep. We'll need the
rest, but I don't know if I can after the vision
with crossbows and learning about a new
possession possibility. I might be able to

possess without touching someone because Dave might have powers of his own. I must be more worn out than I realize because I drift off before too long.

Dave's alarm wakes us up, but we decide to play hooky for a day. We sit close together by the firepit, rehashing memories.

"Remember when Cormac and Molly almost got kicked out of the fair at the end of summer?" I ask.

"Yeah, guess it's against the rules to use it as a place to make out and hold up the line forever." Dave mocks a look of shock.

We both laugh, thinking of our two friends.

"Remember when Ben put Sue in her place?" he asks me.

"Wasn't she saying something bigoted as per usual?"

"Yeah, but Ben and Kyle put her in her place."

The fair had been such a lovely time. Back before our town was haunted. Before a murder victim was found in our borders.

Cormac and Molly were getting along. But it was also before Dave and I could touch. After our day gallivanting around his property, Dave and I fall to sleep free of any nightmares. We're closer together this time and allow a touch to sneak through every now and then.

In the morning, we both need to head into the dock for work. I wish we could just spend more time at his place instead. A memory of him removing his shirt before we went on the kayaks as teens surfaces, and I'm instantly hit with a longing to touch him again. It had taken my breath away when he'd advanced the two steps closing the distance between us at my house and held me. I want to revisit that euphoric feeling. I want to grab him and release this tension. I want to feel the tingling of his touch again.

Driving in together after we're both ready feels different than when he picks me up from my place, in a good way. There's chatter all around as we head our separate directions once he parks his truck. Most of it is about a fire on the island last night. I hadn't heard a thing about it. Molly was working at the bar. She should have at least heard about it. Why didn't she call me? Samhain's tonight so maybe she's busy but still.

The day seems to trudge by, but I've got a smile plastered on my face just about the entire time. Part of me feels like a fool for it, but the other is glad. I seem to sell more cockles throughout this shift. As I'm closing up shop a bit early, I hear something that has my interest piqued.

"They identified the body from Bethel's Landing," one of the guys from Dave's crew says.

"No way," another responds.

"You're shitting me! Who was it?"

The first guy shrugs. "Some chick from out of town. Said she seemed to be some kind of artsy hippie."

With my heart pounding in my chest, I want to grab him by the arm before he can walk away. "Do you know her name?" The guy looks at me curiously but shrugs. Someone else gets a hold of him and starts asking a bunch of questions at the same time making it hard for either one of us to hear each other through all the commotion going on around us. We eventually break free from the crowd, Dave arriving just in time to stop the guy from his crew who announced the finding. Dave asks me what's wrong with a look of concern on his face.

"They identified the body."

Dave's expression changes immediately. "Who is it?"

I swallow hard. "I don't know, but they said she was from out of town. I guess she's an artistic hippie. I wonder why she was in Ethel?"

"Jenny?"

"Yeah, that's her name," the guy from Dave's crew says.

"Our old roommate?" Thinking of her brings back so many memories. Remembering how our garden has never been so good since she moved out has a pang hitting my belly. She can't be dead. Why? She's harmless.

"Kind of sounds like her, right?"

"That's just too close to home."

"Yeah, plus the visions."

"Could Cormac or Ben be next?" Was killing Jenny a way to get to Molly and me? It's not right. She was so sweet always. She constantly had her long hair down and wore sandals, no matter the temp. It's just not fair. Even though she was never a fan of staying in one spot long, she was rooted in our memories. I can't believe we'll never have another visit from her again.

We both take off, running back toward Dave's truck. I feel like everything is moving in slow motion as I try to keep up with him. Then he's speeding out onto the street toward Cormac's house, which is only about ten minutes away, depending on how fast you drive there. Dave parks on Cormac's street, and I'm out of the truck almost before it stops moving. Dave grabs me by the arm, but let's go quickly on my way in-side Cormac's house, and it's enough to stop me but luckily not cause me to possess his soul. "We've got to be smart about this."

I nod with a serious expression, certain I will regret not doing something crazy like barging into Cormac's house if she or Ben were hurt or worse. Cormac opens the door with slow movements looking extremely tired. Her eyes are bloodshot yet glassy along with dark circles. She looks like a walking zombie in Cormac's clothes.

"What happened?" Dave asks Cormac, looking her over once more before turning his eyes on me with a worried stare. Cor-mac explains the situation and what she re-members happening, but it all seems to be coming from a long way off. Her voice sounds distant and muffled as I focus on Cormac again. I can't believe someone broke into her apartment. She claims that it appears nothing's been taken even though the place is ransacked. What were they looking for? Cormac's still talking—something about alerting the authorities.

"So, they don't know who did this yet? How can that be possible? This is Ethel, for crying out loud," I say in disbelief. Cormac looks at the ground when I make eye contact with her before glancing my way apologetically, then down again, avoiding eye contact all together. Then it dawns on me. "Hey, where's Molly?"

"She's at your place," Cormac bites out.

Dave pulls me aside, appearing nervous about Cormac's behavior. "Hey, I think Cormac needs to be alone for now. Can you go home and talk to Molly or something?" Dave asks with hopeful eyes for me to agree so Cormac can be left alone. I'm not sure why he feels the need to defend Cormac, and, even though my heart is beating fast, wanting answers, I nod in agreement.

"Okay," Cormac responds with a bit of relief in her voice, making me wonder what she really thinks about all of this. What is she hiding?

"I'm just going to walk home," I tell Dave as soon as we're outside. I need to think through everything we've just learned. "But then we're going to Ben's, all right?"

"Good," he says. "Meet you at The Daily Grind."

I nod, and we walk in opposite directions. I turn back once to watch him go. I miss Boomer's bark when I walk into our house. We left him at Dave's with Nessa. "Molly?"

I walk through the house and to her room before yelling again, "Molly?"

Panic begins to set in as I make my way back downstairs. Were we wrong thinking the targets were Cormac and Ben?

"What?" she asks as she enters through the back door while pulling boxing gloves off her hands. She must have been punching the bag we have hung out back.

"I couldn't find you."

"Sorry." She shrugs with a frustrated huff.

"What are you so upset about?"

"Cormac blames me for her house being broken into."

"Why?"

"She says I distract me—that I should trust her and let her work with Oliver because it's important."

"I thought you two had made up."

"So did I."

"Want to come with Dave and me? We're going to Ben's house to be sure he's okay. Not only are you having visions of Cormac bound, Dave and I had a vision about Ben being captured."

"Yes. Let's go."

She locks up behind us. "Dave's at The Daily Grind."

"We'll get him and be on our way."

It's almost four in the afternoon when we get there. "Dave," Molly calls, waving her arms frantically.

Dave lifts his head while in a seat at one of the outside cafe tables, looking confused at first seeing Molly instead of me, then relieved to see both of us together.

"You guys want some coffee before we go?" he asks, sipping his coffee and watching for my response over the top of his cup. People walk past behind him nodding or smiling in greeting as they smell something delectable coming from inside The Grind, like fresh baked bread or cookies.

"We don't really have time, do we?" I ask.

But Claire, the barista, shows up just then and says, "I'll be right back with your drinks. The regular?" When I nod yes, she gives me an unsure smile looking at where Molly is sitting then walks inside to put in our orders.

"Can we have ours to go and another paper cup so Dave can take his too?" I ask when she returns.

"We think it's safer if we all go together," I continue studying Dave's face trying to read how he feels about the situation. He leans forward, placing both hands around his mug on the table, staring into its dark depths as though wishing for something more than just coffee. Dave flips his wrist up, checking his watch.

Finally, we're on our way to Ben's. I spot the massive anchor on the front lawn first. Passing the blue sign and ascending the porch steps, I sincerely hope our good friend is okay.

Dave's the first one at the door. "Ben?"

Molly's walking back and forth on the porch peeking into each window as we wait.

Relief hits me when I hear the door creak open and see Ben. "What are you guys doing here?"

Molly hugs him and then clears her throat. "Hey… so about the tux… I need the style number so I can order mine—it's going to take them time to locate one my size and tailor it."

Ben laughs. Dave and I exchange a happy glance.

"I'll get you that number as soon as I can, but you know you should really be more worried about your costume measurements given what today is."

"You're right, Ben," I say. "Dave, can you drive us back to our place?"

"Sure." He gives Ben a friendly slap on the arm. "Glad you're okay, man."

"Me, why wouldn't I be."

With that, Ben's back to work, Dave's driving home to change, and Molly and I are preparing for the gathering before the festival. "Maybe Cormac will forgive me after seeing this costume." Molly looks at me with pleading eyes, and I can't help but roll mine.

*****

I hear the music as we approach the secret spot. It's not all pointy hats, and long dresses as some may assume. There's plenty of modern-day fashion mixed in with the old. Many of our attendees are young and hip. Even those who aren't dress with a sense of style. It is the gathering after all, not just for those who know about it but also for those yet to come into their own power.

My heart beats wildly as we walk closer, toward the crowd. I freeze at the sight before me—a beautiful girl with long blonde hair braided down her back and wearing a gorgeous purple bustier that reminds me of something a princess would wear. Molly gasps next to me, "I love your top! Who made it?"

The girl turns around. I look down, knowing my cheeks are beet red, but when Molly grabs my hand, I look up to see the most beautiful bustier front of deep blues and greens embroidered onto the purple. "I made it. Do you like it?"

"Yes, it's fabulous."

Molly and I keep going. I think there are more people here than ever before. Just as I'm about to ask Molly what she thinks of the crowd, I hear someone behind me say, "It's okay."

I turn back around. The beautiful blonde girl is staring at me with a knowing look on her face. She nods and walks past us, disappearing into the sea of people. We stop every so often to chat with friends or admire clothing. That's when I spot the Gorta. Even dressed in modern clothes, he still has the ancient, powerful feel about him, which makes me stand just a bit straighter when he's nearby. He doesn't notice us right away because he's talking to an older gentleman wearing a hat and carrying a cane. They both stop mid-conversation when they see us staring at them. The old man smiles and tips his hat at Molly and me before walking away.

"To what do I owe the honor," the broody-looking Gorta ironically named Gordan says. "Wait a minute; you two have met your partners."

Molly and I glance at each other and then look back at Gordan. Gortas are often tall and gangly. They surfaced during the horrific Irish famine. They look starved, but their power gives them the ability to feed entire populations. They don't just feed in forms of food but also spiritually. Which is why I think Gordan has been able to pick up on Molly and I's current relationship status.

"Yes, we did." Molly smiles up at Gordan, who rubs his chin in thought.

"After you and yours get through this current fight and a much larger obstacle, you'll be bonded for life."

Molly's smile grows. "Cormac and I, bonded."

Gordan smiles back, making his cheekbones even more pronounced. Then he turns to me.

"You and yours are soulmates. He'll allow your power to grow. Together you'll be an unstoppable force, but you need to connect more; otherwise, the anger will take him over."

"Wait, that's why Dave's been so angry lately? He needs the soul possessing outlet."

Gordan nods. I give Molly an urgent look wanting to get to Dave as quickly as possible. We nod back to Gordan, silently thanking him, but as we're walking away, Molly turns back. "What did you mean by a much larger obstacle?"

"You can't exactly bond with her if she's dead now, can you?" Gordan waves bye and turns to approach others while Molly huffs.

Well, it looks like Dave needs soul possession just when we absolutely must use it to save Cormac.

CHAPTER TWELVE – MOLLY

"May joy and peace surround you, contentment latch your door. And happiness be with you now and bless you evermore."
— An Irish Blessing

Everyone should be heading to the festival, but I'm hoping Dave's still at his house because that's where Orla and I are headed. Cormac wasn't at her house when we stopped, and we didn't see her at the festival. If I wasn't so freaked out, I might be able to celebrate that Dave and Orla can work together to alleviate Dave's anger issues. I sincerely hope the powers do work in tandem like Orla says they did for Ben. We need to see what Oliver is up to with Cormac before it's too late.

I take a seat on the swing, petting Boomer and Nessa. "I'll give you two a minute."

"Thank you." Orla opens the door and enters.

I watch them through the open window, happy for my friend when Dave takes her hand and they sit on the couch. He puts pillows between them, respecting the distance she's always preferred their entire lives. Despite the sadness looming around me, I'm pleased they can finally close the gap. She moves the pillows, and I don't have to be a lipreader to be able to know that she's whispered that they can touch. Their powers will work together, and his irritation can dissipate. I just hope Orla reminds him to think about Cormac when they touch. It's kind of a weird wish to have.

Orla does me a favor and narrates everything she sees aloud. "Oliver and a group of people are preparing for the festival. They all have costumes on. Some of them appear to be dressed as pheasants with aprons while others are more like soldiers with different colors and metal armor."

Those are different costumes than I've seen before. Was there a theme decided upon that I'm unaware of?

"Wait, Oliver's giving instructions. It's so weird - like he's a leader of some sort. He's speaking only to the ones dressed as soldiers. Wait, no, now he's speaking to the pheasants - who are undercover soldiers."

She takes a deep, shaky breath. I find myself worried for my friend. Dave must sense it too. "I can narrate for a while and give you a rest." He must be able to see what Orla sees.

"Oliver's giving orders about what to do if the people resist. It's so weird. I knew he was a successful crew leader, but this is something altogether different. There's more people."

"That's because it's not the Oliver you, know," this comes from a new voice on the porch. It's Gordan. What's he doing here? "I could tell you two were in over your head."

"Should I have Orla come out here too? Dave's in there."

"No, let's not interrupt them. They look adorable, don't they? I'll have plenty of time to meet the newest member."

Oh, that's right. Dave has no idea what he's in for. I pat the swing next to me, inviting Gordan to sit down with me.

"Let me tell you what I can," Gordan says after he takes a seat. "What you saw before was Oliver under the control of Cromwell. He wasn't actually thinking for himself back then so it didn't really count. Now that Cromwell has possessed him fully, it will be something else entirely to unseat him from command of his army. We believe Oliver intends to use them in an attack on this town and surrounding areas. He plans on leaving nothing but ruins behind in his rampage for power. Cormac is our last obstacle in preventing that from happening tonight if we don't act now. The battle won't even be close to fair if she stays under his spell. You two need to convince her to come with you and then take her somewhere safe where she'll be out of harm's way.

"Once no other powers remain, we can deal with Oliver together. He can't wield those weapons if only humans are allowed near them. None of those people know what they really boxed up or where it came from except for Cormac since she was the last one to touch them before they were stuck inside a wall. The soldiers must have been wearing gloves at all times as well as their pheasant costumes so that none of us could sense them through touch or smell alone. We just didn't think to realize that special care needed to be taken when holding shiny weapons or wearing shiny armor. Apparently, Cromwell never thought to inform Oliver of the precautions he needed to take either."

I know where I've seen Cromwell before. The siege of Drogheda was directed by him. This is all part of the visions I've been having. Hearing Cormac is the key, and remembering her being prepared for

157

execution in my visions puts me on edge. Oliver can't be allowed to carry out his plans. Ethel can't take a siege like Drogheda.

"If this works, Ethel will go up in flames just like Ireland did hundreds of years ago." I bring my knees to my chest and draw them into a tight hug for strength.

The metal armor makes sense now too. It's something Cromwell could hold on to with his powers, ensuring that Oliver didn't lose touch with him while absorbed in leading the assault. Was Gordan really there at Drogheda?

Gordan pats my arm. "We won't let a siege like that ever happen again. Do you see now why Oliver must be stopped?"

"So much," I admit to him. That's what I've been trying to explain to Orla. Ethel is in danger, but there are bigger issues at stake if things here go as Cromwell plans them to tonight. "How do we make Cormac come with us? Orla can hop into her head easily enough but getting her out is another story."

Gordan nods and stands up, gesturing for me to follow him off the porch to a patch of dirt where he can draw with a stick. "Oliver has grown to like Cormac. He'll be hesitant to part with her if she stays by his side. If he senses that we mean to take her from him, you might not get another chance."

"I think Cormac would help us if she could, but how can we break a spell by the person who holds the same power as the one who organized the siege of Drogheda."

Gordan points at a line he draws in the dirt. "Here is Bethel's Landing. You and Orla are together here, both on Ethel soil." He circles a spot close to us with big loops of his stick. "Oliver was right about one thing when he said that she's helping them out at sea, and this is the main spot."

He leans down and scratches out another line from Bethel's Landing straight across where Gordan made his large loops.

"We need Orla and you on dock land here, on the other side of the harbor."

Dave yells out so we go back to the porch by the open window. "We can see Cormac now. She stopped watching Oliver and looked down at herself."

"Is she okay?" I ask.

"She's alive and unharmed," Orla reassures me.

"But she's bound by rope," Dave says.

It's just like in my visions. My body begins to visibly shake. "Oh, no."

Why can't I see what they're seeing? Waiting to hear what's going on is awful.

"She's not the only one tied in rope."

"Who else is bound?"

"It's Ben." Now Orla's on the porch. "They blacked out, and we lost our connection."

"It's just like the spirit in the house that bound us when I tried to tell you I'm a banshee," I say to Dave as he joins the rest of us.

"Can it be connected?" he asks.

"You're half banshee." Gordan raises an eyebrow.

"That's semantics." Orla looks exasperated with Gordan.

"Tell me more about the spirit," Gordan says to me, ignoring Orla's correction.

"It carried Dave and I to this hidden room in the house and bound us."

"It was so creepy and giggled as a way of taunting us."

"Something similar happened to me too. The strength of the spirit was like nothing I've felt before," Orla says.

"I must see this room." Gordan drapes his jacket over his shoulder and walks toward Dave's truck.

"Uh, don't we need to get Cormac and Ben before we worry about some spirit?" I grab Gordan's arm.

"The spirit is the key to how Cromwell has been able to have such a tie with Oliver." He pulls me back and points in the direction of the truck. "Your house is the central location for everything that's been

161

going on. I can feel it in my bones. We need to go there now and reclaim your property before Cromwell uses it again against you."

Dave walks up to his truck and opens the passenger side door, catching Gordan's attention.

Before getting in Dave's truck, Orla clears her throat claiming the front passenger seat. Gordan and I get in the back. Boomer hops in the bed with Nessa not too far behind.

"So tell me where we're going," Gordan says.

Dave signals and pulls out onto the main road. "I'm taking you into town."

Ironically, Orla and I have invited full blood supernaturals to our house every year for some time now. We always tried to spruce up the place before the Festival of Samhain. And now, the only year we've been too preoccupied, we finally have a visitor.

Of course, Gordan walks in like he owns the place. He follows some weird

162

sense that I can't determine and goes directly to the hidden door. It's not so hidden now, with the boards haphazardly blocking the entrance. "Can you please remove these? I need in there."

Orla, Dave, and I don't have to go too far as we never had time to put the necessary tools away. With all of us working together, we have access to the haunted room again in no time. Dave passes out flashlights to Gordan and I. He and Orla have one to share.

"You all heard it?" Gordan steps into the room, and we hold our breath waiting for what will happen. "You guys can breathe, you know. I put up a ward against the spirit."

"Can you teach us how to do that?" Orla asks.

"Sure, but first point me to the book." Gordan's shining this flashlight in a pattern, searching the perimeter.

"How do you know about that? Oh, right. It was over in that corner, but after the voice and everything, I'm not sure what happened to it." Orla points her flashlight to the corner, and sure enough, there it is.

"The key's in this diary." Gordan's already flipping through the pages.

"What key?" I ask.

"The key to how Oliver will be signaled that it's time."

CHAPTER THIRTEEN – ORLA
"As you slide down the banisters of life,
may the splinters never point the wrong
way."

As we round the corner, I see the mayday
signal from the lighthouse. It's exactly as
the diary said it would be. Next, we hear
gunshots from the island warning of in-
vaders like they did in the historic Drogheda reports. Fisherfolk are all assembled
along the coast, their candlelight glimmer-
ing off the water. The way the Festival of
Samhain traditions are playing right into
this macabre reunion of sorts is disturbing.

A loud, ghostly howl echoes through
the air, freezing everyone in their place. It
sounds like it's coming from the lighthouse
though it's a bit hard to decipher given that
we're hearing it through truck windows.

"What the Dubnos is that?" Gordan
tries to shield his eyes from the light.

"I don't know, but I don't like it." Dave
grips the steering wheel tightly.

We all sit there paralyzed by fear as another howl echoes through the air. This time, it sounds closer and more ominous.

Then we see it – a shadowy figure emerging from the lighthouse, it's Oliver but it's also not Oliver. The howl seems to come from the demon currently haunting him, Cromwell.

"Floor it!" Molly screams as Dave veers toward the pier. I hope she's not hearing ringing.

As we drive, the figure's gaze follows us, its howls growing louder and more frenzied. We can see the other fisherfolk up ahead, their candles providing some measure of safety.

Cormac comes into view. Molly's breath hitches, her light providing a beacon of hope. I'm about to speak when I feel something sharp digging into my skin – Gordan's fingernails digging into my arm tightly but not to the point where skin makes contact, avoiding possession.

"Don't let her," he whispers at me as we drive as close as we can to the lighthouse.

I feel a tugging sensation, and then I'm out of the car, running toward the light. The others are following behind me. I spot Ben's Crestliner docked and available. Where is he? I look at Dave, and we both return our gazes to Ben's boat, eyes wide. He hops in to start it while I untie the middle. Molly nods at Gordan directing him to follow her while she boards. Given the current, I untie the bow next. After that, I untie the stern, let the boat drift the way I'd anticipated, and hop on. My hands are shaking, but I'm glad to have been able to accomplish a task, no matter how many times I've done it before. This is different, more urgent. Dave smiles at me; despite everything, we work well as a team. His warmth allows me to regain my strength.

As we near, the figure becomes clearer. It's Oliver, but he's covered in armor. He's wearing a shiny breastplate and helmet.

The howl seems to come from within him, but it's not his voice.

"Oliver!" I scream as we run to him. Approaching the lighthouse foundation, I'm taken aback by how much it reminds me of the Drogheda medieval curtain wall.

He reaches for me, but the spirit of Cromwell pulls him back, laughing maniacally.

"You can't have her," he yells. "She's mine!"

A massive flame roars to life. The townspeople have ignited the festival bonfire, but it's as if they, too, are in a trance like Oliver. A muffled shriek cries out from above, and I see where Cormac has been moved to. She's on the lighthouse catwalk. Ben is next to her. They're both on their knees, hands bound behind their backs, and gags around their heads. Three hooded figures are behind them. The fear I've had for everyone lately begins festering to rage.

"Their shrieks are the same pitch as my ringing," Molly says. "I can't tell if there's ringing inside my head right now." Molly falls to the ground, gasping for breath through shock hyperventilation. Gordan runs over and helps her up.

Molly's ringing would be louder than their shrieks based on her descriptions. I hope that means something good, I really hope. Looking back up, I'm relieved to see that Oliver isn't going to attempt to hang Cormac and Ben. Instead, he's given orders from down here to the three in hoods up there. They escort our friends back inside the lantern room and appear to lead them down the spiral staircase.

I need to attempt an execution ritual if the diary studies are accurate. I'm not sure why it was referred to as an execution ritual, as it's more like an exorcism. Cromwell has taken Oliver – our Oliver – hostage, and we need to bring him back. We need to do this before anything happens to Cormac or Ben.

Dave, Gordan, and Molly all give me knowing looks. I'm glad Molly's recovered, and she and Gordan are back fighting this evil. We pull out the items we need for the ritual and step closer to the lighthouse.

As we reach the lighthouse, I can hear Cromwell's laughter ringing in my ears. We set up quickly, and I begin the ritual. Rope just like from our visions and what's been used to tie Cormac and Ben's hands, is one of our essential items. Another is a few claddagh rings. Finally, we have lavender. I string four pieces of rope through four claddagh rings and tie a knot holding the lavender and each ring securely. Handing one to Dave, I nod, and he nods back. I hand one each to Molly and Gordan glad that he's helped her get a grip. It pains me to see the red around her eyes from crying. One is left for me. It's difficult to concentrate with the howling, and laughing, but we need to focus.

"What are you doing?" Oliver cries out.

"Saving you," I reply.

I can see the confusion in his eyes and then the moment of realization. He knows what's happening. He fights against Cromwell, but it's no use; the demon is too strong.

"You have to let me go," he shouts at us.

"I'm sorry, we can't do that," Molly says as we begin the ritual.

The light begins to flicker, and then the howling stops.

"I to the waves lift mine eyes, from whence doth come my harmony…" we say in unison, and Ben visibly begins shaking. We need to call Jenny's spirit for help, but I had no idea it would affect him so strongly. "We need your help, friend."

"Why?" A wind carrying Jenny's words rushes through the group and knocks Cormac over. "They killed me!"

"Don't you want revenge?" With this, Oliver begins twitching as if creepy, crawling things are slithering all over his skin.

All four of us hold out the rope, ring, and lavender pieces in front of us and recite, "leave this world, Cromwell, You're not welcome."

The three hooded figures burst into dust. Flames leap out of the bonfire catching the grass and spreading as if gasoline surrounds us all. It's so close the heat warms my face. Both Cormac and Ben begin floating in the air. Some of the people who had been holding candles earlier but didn't help ignite the bonfire have now approached the island holding their flames out as if to build onto the pyre. Gordan falls to his knees, dropping his rope, ring, and lavender piece to the ground.

"You okay?" I ask.

Molly checks his vitals and picks up the rope before it is caught by the fire.

"I must starve them of the evil and feed them with good," Gordan says.

He looks around at the townsfolk who have joined our little gathering as he says this. I search their eyes in terror, hoping to see any sign that it's working. We don't have time for delay.

"Good, you're finally preoccupied again," Cromwell's voice seethes through Oliver.

Ben and Cormac are shaking. What's happening?

"Molly? How's Gordan doing?"

"He's so gaunt."

"He's always gaunt," Dave interjects.

"It's okay. I almost have all of them," Gordan says.

Eventually, light enters the townsfolks' eyes, and they no longer hold zoned-out gazes.

Molly helps Gordan back to his feet, and we continue where we left off.

"Leave this world, Cromwell. You're not welcome," we wail a little louder.

Ben and Cormac are levitated directly over the bonfire. A platform with two posts appears out of nowhere. Their bodies are lowered at just the right angle for their hands to lock them around the poles. If they're brought down to the podium, they'll be burnt at the stake. The flames grow higher. Our time is running out.

Molly and Gordan clasp their free hands together and step forward. Dave grabs my hand. He's thinking of Cromwell, like we discussed. I possess Cromwell's soul instantaneously. Visions of his secret lover who had traveled to Drogheda ahead of him in order to ascertain classified intelligence filter in. She had been the love of his life, but the last letter he received from her said she'd caught a deadly illness and didn't believe she'd make it another week. He didn't get there in time. When he saw her corpse, he went mad. Viewing it through his memories is terrifying.

I feel the connection between Dave and I deepening, gaining more control like a partnership, our powers intermingling. So I think of Jenny and he's possessing her soul, as she gives us the final vital step we need.

"Throw the rope into the fire," Dave says, and we all do.

I look at Molly. "No ringing," she says, and I know we can move forward.

"Leave this world, Cromwell. You're not welcome," we scream at the top of our lungs.

Then, Oliver's body falls to the ground, and the fire disappears completely, leaving us in the dark. I hear a whisper in Jenny's voice. "He's gone. Peace be with you." For a moment, I see her silhouette floating away into the night over the ocean and earth she so loved in life.

"Thank you, Jenny. Be at peace forever more."

Dave carries Oliver, who's unresponsive to the boat. Gordan and Molly hover over him for a second, trying to assess the damage. Gordan shrugs his shoulders and then turns to check Ben, quickly sending us a thumbs up as Ben rises, rubbing his neck and wrists. Molly rushes over to Cormac to be sure she's okay. Apart from having a few bruises and looking rightfully pissed,

Cormac appears healthy. That was close, inexplicably close.

"She's going to be okay," I say quietly. "Just give her some time."

We all sit there in the boat in silence, our thoughts consumed with what we've just been through. But we're all alive, and that's what matters. As long as we're together, we can face anything.

The Festival of Samhain is supposed to be a time of joy and celebration, but this year it's been anything but.

"Let's go. We need to get him out of here," Dave says urgently.

"We should take Oliver to urgent care for the burns," I say, and everyone nods in approval. "I think Ben and Cormac should be checked, too, just in case. They might have smoke inhalation." This is met with Cormac rolling her eyes, Molly nudging her to follow orders, and the two wrapped up in each other's arms.

"Can I use your phone?" Ben asks. "I need to call Kyle."

After docking, Dave carries Oliver into Urgent Care, and we all follow. Since he's the one in the most distraught state, he's checked first. We all sigh a breath of relief when his vitals appear okay. They need further testing, but I'm very hopeful.

"Go, you two," Gordan says. "We can handle it from here."

"Yeah," Molly nervously snickers. "Did you know that you two glowed when you joined hands? You should go somewhere private and check that out." Cormac winks and then kisses Molly.

We both shake our heads but do as we're bid. Walking to my house with Dave, I'm finally able to slow my heart rate. We did it. We rid this town of its ghost. We hold hands the entire way without possessing each other's souls. Dave kisses my forehead, and we stop on the sidewalk. As he turns to me my heart rate ticks up again but this time in excitement, not fear. He moves a piece of hair out of my eyes and cups my chin. I look up at him as he leans down to me, and our lips meet, and there's heat. We move our chins rhythmically, falling deeper into the kiss each time. Now my breathing is ragged. Once there's a pause, we smile and walk the rest of the way home as quickly as we can.

*****

As soon as we're inside, he's grabbing my hair as our bodies are like magnets pulling us into one another. Then he moves one hand to my hip and the other to the nape of my neck while he kisses below my ear on the opposite side. I gasp, and so does he. This isn't in our mind because now we're free to touch without soul possession. This is for real. I lift my head, giving him more access to my throat, and moan. There's the tingling sensation on my hip where he's touching that I knew would be there. It's everything I've hoped for and more.

He pulls away slightly, both of his hands on my face. Our eyes meet, and I can see the love and desire in his. "You feel so good," I tell him breathlessly.

He smiles at me and kisses me again, this time slower and with more intensity. We touch each other everywhere because we finally can. His hands move down my back to my butt and he squeezes gently before moving them around to the front and pulling me against him. I can sense him against me, and it feels so good after wanting him for so long. I moan again into his mouth as he deepens the kiss.

We finally break apart, both of us gasping for air. Dave looks at me with such love and admiration that I feel like I could burst. "I've wanted to do that for a very long time."

"Me too," I reply honestly.

He kisses me again, and we start walking toward the bedroom. We touch each other the whole way there, not able to get enough of each other. We fall onto the bed together, and Dave undresses me. I do the same to him, and when we're both nude, we just look at each other.

"You're so beautiful," Dave whispers as he caresses my cheek gently.

I blush at his words, and Dave leans in to kiss me again. This time, the kiss is slow and full of love. He moves his hand down my body to my center and starts stroking me gently. I moan and arch my back, wanting more. Dave obliges by slipping a finger inside of me and moving it around skillfully. The pleasure is building quickly, and I cry out as I come. Dave kisses me through my orgasm and then moves up to lie beside me.

"I love you," he whispers as he starts to kiss down my body.

I shiver in anticipation as Dave moves down between my legs. He starts licking and sucking on my center, sending bolts of pleasure through me. I come again quickly, and Dave moves up to join me once more.

"I love you, Orla," Dave tells me as he kisses me passionately. "I love you so much."

"I love you too," I say out of breath.

Then he places an elbow on each side of my head, kissing me while our warm bodies press against each other. It's intense as he enters but not all the pain I'd imagined the first time. I put my arms around his shoulders, feeling the taut muscles. His back flexes with his movements as my body tightens around him and threatens to explode yet again. The back and forth motion that follows has me riveted in pleasure.

We make love until the early hours of the morning, finally falling asleep in each other's arms, content knowing that we're finally together and can be together forever.

CHAPTER FOURTEEN – MOLLY

"May the Irish hills caress you.
May her lakes and rivers bless you.
May the luck of the Irish enfold you.
May the blessings of Saint Patrick behold
you."

A perfect hue of beige roses, white drapery, and sturdy mahogany surrounds us as if Kyle and Ben's dream wedding board came to life. It's their special day, and I couldn't be happier. Walking Cormac down the aisle sends happy shivers down my spine. I know we're just bests, but I can imagine her in white someday walking down the aisle toward me. Ben grins at me as he starts to say his vows, and I can see the love in his eyes as he gazes at Kyle. Everything is immaculate. The ceremony goes by quickly, and soon, Ben and Kyle are husbands.

Exiting Ethel Manor past the huge columns and down the brick sidewalk feels like a different time and place. We head to the reception hall, and the party is already in full swing. Ben and Kyle disappear into a corner with some other locals while I circulate around the room, talking to everyone. I'm so happy that they could all be here to celebrate with us and that our town is no longer haunted. Even Oliver has recovered enough to attend though we're still working out things with the police force. Hopefully, everything will be overturned in light of his actions were not quite his for a time. He's slow dancing with Claire, and I think the two (at least the old Oliver and our most talented barista) will make a great pair.

I dance with Ben first and then Kyle, both of them spinning me around expertly. Cormac eventually saves me, taking me away for a slow dance. We make our way to the buffet table and start piling food onto our plates. Cormac kisses me after taking a bite of chicken, and I can taste the BBQ sauce on her lips. I never would have guessed that BBQ could be an aphrodisiac, but it sure enough is. I imagine her in a robe again, seated on her bath step while I run water. I kiss her neck softly and wrap my arms around her waist. She giggles and raises her eyebrows, letting me know this should wait until later.

Orla and Dave are sitting with us. They haven't been able to take their hands off each other. I'm so happy for my friend. She doesn't have to be alone anymore. She's found a human she's free to touch without being plagued by her power. I've yet to secure such control on mine. But I'm so glad that now we can live life free of horrific visions. Orla plans to move in with Dave, and Cormac plans to move in with me. They can keep their fish smell, and we'll keep our Guinness aroma, but I'm going to miss her. We did run through a complete protection practice of our house, ridding it of any more poltergeist activity from the hidden room.

Ben and Kyle join us for a bit and what they have to share is unbelievable.

"I've restored old photos our ancestors brought over here from Ireland," Ben says while pushing his glasses higher on the bridge of his nose.

"His work is amazing," Kyle says. "Take a look. It's like they're brand new."

Ben kisses Kyle, their different color tuxes complementing each other and perfectly sculpted hair making a photogenic moment. It should be saved forever. Their love is one for the books, for sure.

Ben pulls out a photo and hands it to Orla. Her face flushes, and the hand that doesn't hold the photo grips the seat of her chair in a vice-like death hold. I take the photo out of her hands. It's of a couple. The man eerily looks like the vision of the ghost who had possessed Oliver. He has a defined nose that looks as if the brows above are in a constant scrunch. His hair is shoulder length, parted down the middle, and he has a short, stubbly beard. What catches my eye most though, is the woman his gaze has fallen on—it's Jenny, but from a long time ago.

"Do you think?" Orla asks me.

"After what we've been through, I'm beginning to think many more things are possible."

"When we possessed Cromwell's soul," Orla says while pointing to the man in the photo, "I saw visions of his secret lover who had traveled to Drogheda ahead of him in order to ascertain classified intelligence filter. She had been the love of his life, but the last letter he received from her said she'd caught a deadly illness and didn't believe she'd make it another week. He didn't get there in time. When he saw her corpse, he went mad."

Dave has his arm around Orla's shoulders and squeezes her trapezius in comfort. "Yeah, but the vision of the woman was unclear. We couldn't make out who she was."

I point to the woman who looks like Jenny in the photo. "No wonder she was an integral part in ridding our town of Cromwell."

"You don't say," Kyle barks. "You know, you guys could have asked me to help you the night of Samhain. I do leave the bar for emergencies, damn it."

We all promise Kyle never to leave him in the dark again. Gordan's left town now but will return next year. It was easy enough to hide powers and magic from Ben since he was in such a state of shock during the whole ordeal, but there's no way Kyle wouldn't have picked up on something otherworldly had he hung out with the Gorta. Cormac and I finish our plates and head out to the gazebo for some alone time before the night is over.

As we dance under the twinkling starlight, she intertwines her fingers with mine, "I never asked you. How did you get out to Bethel's landing before we did the night they found the body?"

I lean back to take a look at her. "Dave called us. It's a small town." I don't know where she's going with this.

"You don't have a connection to the ones in the afterlife like I do?"

"Well—"

"Tell me."

Letting out an exasperated breath, I acquiesce. "I hear ringing when death is near."

Cormac's face lights up. "You're a half banshee!"

"Yes, how do you know that?"

"Oh, I had camp with one."

Small world. Where's she going with this? I still don't know.

"I was able to compliment her ability a little."

"What?"

"Yeah, is there anything you'd like to use as target practice?"

I look around, finally spotting some crabgrass. "There." I point to it.

She grabs my hand and begins chanting something. "Now, open your mouth."

I look at her in surprise.

"No, don't look at anything but the weed."

I look back at the crabgrass, Cormac begins chanting again, and I open my mouth. An earsplitting high pitched noise comes out of me like nothing I've heard before. It decimates the weed.

"You compliment my power like Dave compliments Orla's."

"See, they're not the only soul mates."

She smiles, and we kiss a long kiss under the moonlight.

Eventually, we head back inside to the dance floor, where we spend the rest of the night. I can't believe that my life is this perfect and that I get to spend it with the people I love most. As the reception comes to an end, I know that this is only the beginning of a beautiful journey ahead.

THE END

ACKNOWLEDGMENTS

Much thanks to Alicia Dean, Wendy Million, and Amy Brewer who graciously helped me improve my first adult fiction book. They caught things I'd missed, helped me improve wording, and reignited my love of writing. Gratitude also to the ICU staff who saved me. While I continue to suffer from 90 dB tinnitus 24/7 because of the illness, they did save my life and for that I will be ever grateful. And now you know where my inspiration for Molly's power comes from.

More thanks to my fellow Stacked Book Club members. You always bring new books to my attention, keeping my reading fresh. Smart and conversational, they also happen to be some of my favorite dinner companions. Finally, love and appreciation to my family and close friends for supporting me and putting up with my chaotic book habits.

ABOUT THE AUTHOR

Stephanie Hansen is a PenCraft and Global Book Award Winning Author. Her debut novella series, Altered Helix, released in 2020. It hit the #1 New Release, #1 Best Seller, and other top 100 lists on Amazon. It is now being adapted to an animated story for Tales. Her debut novel, Replaced Parts, released in 2021 through Fire & Ice YA and Tantor Audio. It has been in a Forbes article, hit Amazon bestseller lists, and made the Apple young adult coming soon bestsellers list. The second book in the Transformed Nexus series, Omitted Pieces, released in 2022. She is a member of the deaf and hard of hearing community so she tries to incorporate that into her fiction. https://www.authorstephaniehansen.com/